Hetty's World

Alaska in 1897

W N E S

Dyea River

Chilkoot Trail

Finnegans Point

Dyea

The first campsite

Dyea Inlet

Skagway

The Golden Stairs
Chilkoot Pass
Sheep Camp
The Scales
Pleasant Camp
Canada
Alaska
1 2 3 4
Miles

History Mysteries from American Girl:

The Smuggler's Treasure, *by Sarah Masters Buckey*
Hoofbeats of Danger, *by Holly Hughes*
The Night Flyers, *by Elizabeth McDavid Jones*
Voices at Whisper Bend, *by Katherine Ayres*
Secrets on 26th Street, *by Elizabeth McDavid Jones*
Mystery of the Dark Tower, *by Evelyn Coleman*
Trouble at Fort La Pointe, *by Kathleen Ernst*
Under Copp's Hill, *by Katherine Ayres*
Watcher in the Piney Woods, *by Elizabeth McDavid Jones*
Shadows in the Glasshouse, *by Megan McDonald*
The Minstrel's Melody, *by Eleonora E. Tate*
Riddle of the Prairie Bride, *by Kathryn Reiss*
Enemy in the Fort, *by Sarah Masters Buckey*
Circle of Fire, *by Evelyn Coleman*
Mystery on Skull Island, *by Elizabeth McDavid Jones*
Whistler in the Dark, *by Kathleen Ernst*
Mystery at Chilkoot Pass, *by Barbara Steiner*

Mystery at Chilkoot Pass

by

Barbara Steiner

American Girl®

HISTORY MYSTERIES

Published by Pleasant Company Publications

For information, address: Book Editor, Pleasant Company Publications, 8400 Fairway Place, P.O. Box 620998, Middleton, WI 53562.

Printed in the United States of America.
02 03 04 05 06 07 RRD 10 9 8 7 6 5 4 3 2 1

PERMISSIONS & PICTURE CREDITS
The following individuals and organizations have generously given permission to reprint illustrations contained in "A Peek into the Past": p. 157—pamphlet cover, courtesy of Candy Waugaman; pp. 158–159—Dyea beach, MSCUA, University of Washington Libraries, Hegg58; map by Susan McAliley; Golden Stairs, MSCUA, University of Washington Libraries, 1146; pp. 160–161—cart, Alaska State Library / Winter and Pond Collection, PCA 21-13; women on trail, Parks Canada, Department of Canadian Heritage; prospector, MSCUA, University of Washington Libraries, Hegg3223; pan of gold, courtesy of Candy Waugaman; pp. 162–163—Belinda Mulrooney, Courtesy of the Bancroft Library, University of California, Berkeley, BANC MSS 77/81, carton 1:3; laundress, MSCUA, University of Washington Libraries, HeggB461; Jack London, Bettmann/CORBIS; landscape, ©Adrian Dorst.
Author photo, p. 165, Haskell Photography, Denver.

Cover and Map Illustrations: Douglas Fryer
Line Art: Greg Dearth

Library of Congress Cataloging-in-Publication Data

Steiner, Barbara A.
Mystery at Chilkoot Pass / by Barbara Steiner. — 1st ed.
p. cm. — (History mysteries ; 17)
"American girl."
Summary: At the start of the Klondike gold rush of 1897, while traveling through Canada with her father, uncle and friends, twelve-year-old aspiring author Hetty tries to determine the identity of a thief.

ISBN 1-58485-488-X — ISBN 1-58485-487-1 (pbk.)
[1. Gold mines and mining—Fiction. 2. Robbers and outlaws—Fiction. 3. Canada—Fiction. 4. Mysteries and detective stories.]
I. Title. II. Series.
PZ7.S825 My 2001 [Fic]—dc21 2001036972

For Susan Cohen, my super agent,
who found this history/mystery series for me

For Peg Ross, my editor, who helped me find
a better story than I thought possible

TABLE OF CONTENTS

Chapter 1 Alaska 1

Chapter 2 The Tent Restaurant 12

Chapter 3 Sarah Lancaster 28

Chapter 4 On the Trail 36

Chapter 5 More Is Missing 50

Chapter 6 A Bath and Other Entertainment 65

Chapter 7 Sheep Camp 76

Chapter 8 Another Thief 87

Chapter 9 The Golden Stairs 101

Chapter 10 The Blizzard 109

Chapter 11 Danger! 120

Chapter 12 Digging Out 131

Chapter 13 A Fairy-Tale Wedding 136

Chapter 14 Confronting the Thief 145

A Peek into the Past 157

CHAPTER I
ALASKA

Papa!" Hetty McKinley screamed as a rush of people crowded the rope ladders, sending her sprawling on the deck. The steamer rode low in the water, so her father simply picked her up and lowered her over the rail of the ship onto a smaller, flat-bottomed boat he called a scow. She landed with a thud, glanced around, then called back to him, "We're nowhere near shore, Papa."

"Just steady yourself and hang on," Papa shouted.

Hetty's Uncle Donall dropped her best friend, Alma Vasquez, beside her like a sack of potatoes. Alma grabbed Hetty's hand and squeezed her brown eyes tight as the boat rocked.

"Look, Alma, your mother is climbing down that rope." Hetty watched as the plump Maria Vasquez turned loose of the knotted rope and landed beside them. Both girls grabbed her hands to steady her.

"Oh, my goodness, I never dreamed I could do that. But I didn't want us to be separated." Alma's mother laughed instead of being scared like Hetty and Alma as the scow rocked on the choppy waves.

"Here comes a crate, Hetty," Papa yelled. He tried to lower the box slowly, but it fell at Hetty's feet and broke open.

Other passengers from the steamer jumped onto the scow, bumping and pushing Hetty and Alma. In the sea around them, horses snorted and dogs swam for shore. Goats, mules, and oxen splashed and struggled toward the beach, at least a mile away. Sailors threw boxes and trunks from the steamer. Some missed the scow, splashed into the icy water, and sank. Hetty hoped none of those supplies were theirs.

Papa swung over the rail and dropped, light on his feet. Uncle Donall rigged a rope system and lowered more of their provisions into Papa's arms.

"Help me, Hetty, Alma." Mrs. Vasquez was trying to gather supplies around her. The scow was riding so low that water had begun to run over their feet. Moments later, the scow, towed by men in a rowboat, moved away from the steamer they'd traveled on for a week from San Francisco.

"I'll stay here with the rest of our things, Glen," Uncle Donall shouted to Papa. "Come back for another load when the scow returns."

More than half of their supplies were still on the steamer. Hetty, in the endless hours of the trip north, had calculated that they had brought four thousand pounds. Enough to last until next summer—as long as it would take them to make it to Dawson and the goldfields of the Yukon, five hundred miles to the north.

A chilly wind whipped Hetty's dark hair into her face. She pulled it back with both hands so she could look around as the scow moved toward shore. What she saw made her mouth fall open. Mountains, dusted with snow, split the pale blue sky. Ahead was Dyea beach, but there was no wharf, no one to help them unload. They had to help themselves, as did the thousands of other passengers who spilled over each other in their eagerness to find gold.

Dyea, which they'd heard was a boomtown, appeared to be only a few wooden buildings huddled together in the distance. Hetty scanned the rugged horizon beyond, but she couldn't make out Chilkoot Pass, the narrow gap through which they'd cross the mountains from Alaska into Canada. The idea of walking seventeen miles through the mountains to Chilkoot Pass, hauling all their supplies, overwhelmed her imagination. Once they crossed the pass, Hetty knew, they still had to walk down the mountain to Lake Lindeman, set up camp for the winter, and build a boat. Next spring, they would travel along lakes and rivers the rest of the way to Dawson.

Papa touched Hetty's shoulder, bringing her out of her

thoughts. He pointed to where many scows were landing. "Looks like we'll unload right at the water's edge. Take whatever you can carry up to dry ground, beyond reach of the tide. One of you girls must guard our supplies up there while the other helps Maria haul the rest. I'll go back to the ship to help Donall."

"Is it safe, Glen, to leave one of the girls alone?" Maria Vasquez asked. She frowned and shaded her eyes from the weak sunshine.

"I think so. We have no choice. Don't talk to anyone, Hetty."

The scow thumped aground. Papa and the other passengers began to unload boxes and crates. Mrs. Vasquez lifted her small trunk. Hetty stumbled in the wet sand as she stepped off the scow, but she and Alma together grabbed a twenty-five-pound bag of oatmeal and ran for higher ground. Saturated with water, the bag was twice as heavy as it should have been. As Mrs. Vasquez and Alma ran back for another load, Hetty stood guard and watched the tide rising, waves rolling in like a hungry monster heading for their food.

"Your turn, Hetty," Alma said when she returned with another load. "I'll guard. I need to rest."

Hetty dashed back toward the water and lifted a slab of bacon and a bag of dried apricots. She slipped on the muddied sand. A boy about her age grabbed her arm and steadied her. He grinned and hurried on.

When it was her turn to guard again, Hetty leaned on a crate to ease her aching muscles and stared at the scurrying people around her. Down near the water, supplies were piled into mountains. Tents, frying pans, sheet-iron stoves, luggage, bales of hay, coils of rope, shovels, and goldpans—everyone had similar things. Everyone had read the supply lists in the *San Francisco Call.* They had spent their life savings making sure they bought every item. Everything they owned was stacked right here. People scrambled over and between the piles like rats or mice, looking for crates, barrels, or trunks labeled with their names. Hetty saw one man climb on a hill of unclaimed provisions and start to call out names—"Carter, Simmons, Redcliffe." He tossed bags and boxes into waiting arms.

Dogs barked. A goat seemed to laugh at the frenzy around them, but maybe she was scared or needed to be milked. The air filled with gulls, screeching and diving for loose scraps of food.

Hetty saw Alma scramble through the crowd, carrying a big tin of tea. "There are more people on this beach than in the entire city of San Francisco, Alma."

Alma giggled. "Stop exaggerating, Hetty. I agree there must be thousands of people here, but— Look, isn't that Mr. Parker?" Alma pointed to a man they'd met on the steamer. He was sitting closer to the water on a tent roll, crying.

"You watch our things, Alma. When Papa said not to

talk to anyone, he meant a stranger. I'm going to see what's wrong." Hetty ran to the giant man. She and Alma had been afraid of Amos Parker at first. He was nearly seven feet tall and looked fierce until they got to know him. "Mr. Parker, what's the matter?"

Mr. Parker looked up and wiped his eyes. "I've lost everything, Hetty. All two thousand pounds."

He wiped his nose on the sleeve of his dirty red shirt. "Those blasted sailors threw everything off the steamer without a care. What wasn't lost in the water is either broken or wet."

"Are you sure it's all ruined? As soon as Papa gets back, we'll help you carry things to higher ground." Hetty was exhausted, but if Mr. Parker needed help, she would work some more.

"It's too late. Too late. I'll have to go home, although the journey's just starting, although we've just set foot in Alaska. No prospecting for gold for me." Tears ran into Mr. Parker's black beard. Hetty had rarely seen a grown man cry, and certainly not one as huge as Amos Parker.

With a heavy heart, but knowing there was nothing she could do, she ran back to Alma and explained Mr. Parker's dilemma. Wind started to blow, and Hetty bounced to stay warm. The sun was a huge, sparkling dinner plate, but the air was crisp and cold, signaling the coming fall.

It was already the twenty-second of September, 1897.

Papa had wanted to get an earlier start, but all the ships had been booked. From the moment that prospectors stepped off a steamer in San Francisco Bay last July shouting, "Gold, we've found gold in the Yukon!" everyone had wanted to sail north to seek his fortune. Hetty had heard stories about people dropping everything to rush north, mad with gold fever. Bank tellers abandoned their jobs, leaving people standing in line at the counters. Waiters in restaurants left diners at tables without their meals.

Hetty had turned twelve on the day in August when Papa announced they were going to the Yukon to search for gold. Alma had turned twelve the day they'd left San Francisco. What a birthday present!

Hetty rubbed the locket hanging on a chain around her neck, the locket her mother had given her for her eighth birthday. It held the only picture Hetty had of her mother. Would Mama have liked coming on this trip?

Just then Mrs. Vasquez reappeared, a bag of beans on one shoulder, a bag of cornmeal on the other. She laid both at Alma's feet. "Girls, this is the last of our first load. But the scow is back. Glen is unloading more now. Hetty, you stay here. Alma, come help Glen and me."

Hetty wanted to go find Papa, but she knew she had to stand watch. People who had lost everything might decide they could steal supplies that lay unclaimed.

She looked behind her and saw new white tents springing up beside the thousands already pitched near the town of Dyea. A tent city, Hetty thought. A tent city, flags flying, filled with people eager to look for gold.

It took hours to get the rest of their supplies off the steamer onto the scow, to move them off the scow onto the beach, and then to relay their things up the beach to dry ground. From there they had to carry everything again to where they would pitch their tent for the night. Hetty realized this was what they'd have to do again and again to climb up and over the mountain.

By the time the last load was carried to the campsite, her arms ached and her dress was muddy. She wanted to lie down and sleep for hours, but it was only late afternoon and there was still work to do if they were going to start hiking tomorrow. She and Alma leaned on a stack of flour bags. Hetty sighed and looked around.

A flag she had spotted from the beach turned out to be someone's red long underwear. She nudged Alma and pointed, and both girls laughed.

Hetty, Alma, and Papa set up two canvas tents, one for the men and one for the women. Mrs. Vasquez, her face pale with exhaustion, got a fire started, brewed a pot of coffee, and set a pan of water to boil.

"Where is Uncle Donall?" Hetty asked as they pounded the last tent stake into the ground.

"I imagine he's had enough of hard work." Mrs. Vasquez's brown eyes were anxious as she looked over their supplies.

"You think it's all here, Mama?" Alma asked.

"I can't begin to say until I take inventory. Glen, half your goods are wet."

"The last load got soaked by the rising tide. I'm afraid it's ruined." Papa never looked at Hetty as he took out a pipe and tamped it full of tobacco. With a groan, he sat down beside the fire.

"If our food is wet, Papa, will we have to go back home?" Hetty asked.

Papa shook his head. Hetty couldn't tell whether he was saying no, or he didn't know, or he was just too tired to make a decision.

The familiar smell of Papa's pipe blended with smoke from their fire. All around them, campfires crackled and bacon sizzled, sending a tantalizing smell skyward. Dogs barked. Somewhere a fiddler played a merry tune. A current of excitement from the tent city circled Hetty, and the feeling was catching. Hetty's heart beat a little faster, and she collapsed beside Alma on a log they had pulled up near the fire.

They couldn't go back now! At first, Hetty hadn't wanted to run off to the Yukon to hunt for gold. But they'd come this far already—and what if they *could* pick up gold nuggets the size of potatoes? What if they could go back to California as rich as all the snooty people on

Nob Hill? What if she could have all the dresses she wanted and go to fancy parties? What if she and Papa could buy a house with a dozen rooms and indoor bathrooms?

After Mama died, they'd had to sell their small house to pay doctor bills, and Papa had seemed content to live in a couple of rented rooms. Hetty had the big room, but in one corner was their tiny kitchen and a dining table. Her bed was partitioned off with a curtain, giving her a little privacy. But if they had a house, she could have a room of her own. And a desk, her very own desk.

Hetty wanted more than anything else to be a writer. Not a newspaper reporter like Papa, but a writer of novels, like Jane Austen and Charles Dickens. When she had been arguing with Papa, saying that she wouldn't come on this trip, he had told her, "Writers are always curious about what is happening around them. Writers go looking for adventures and stories. The Klondike gold rush is going to be the story of the century, Hetty."

Wouldn't the joke be on her if Papa was right? Hetty smiled, thinking she'd be glad to apologize to Papa. She looked up to see the boy who had helped her on the beach walk by. With him was another boy who was bigger and taller. Hetty caught the older boy's eye and he smiled back at her. But his was not a friendly smile. He looked smug, as if he had read all her thoughts and was laughing at her foolish daydreaming. Hetty watched as the pair faded into the growing darkness, then quickly forgot them.

"Oh, my Lord, no, no, no!" The sound of sobbing followed Mrs. Vasquez's words.

Hetty turned around to see that Mrs. Vasquez had gone inside the tent.

"Mama, what's wrong?" Alma jumped up and rushed inside with Hetty and Papa right behind her.

"My purse, my little red pouch— All my money, all the money I have in the whole world is gone!"

As Hetty's eyes adjusted to the dim light inside the tent, she saw that Mrs. Vasquez had collapsed beside her trunk of personal possessions. The trunk was open, its contents spilling out.

"I thought I got off the boat wearing it around my neck, tucked into my blouse, but just a few moments ago I realized it was gone. Then I thought maybe I had taken it off and hidden it in my trunk. But it's not there, and it's not around my neck."

Mrs. Vasquez started to cry again. Hetty had never seen Mrs. Vasquez so upset. But just like the giant, Amos Parker, Mrs. Vasquez sobbed and tears ran down her face. "We can't go on, Alma. We don't have the money to go on. Our adventure, our chance to be rich, is spoiled. And all through my carelessness."

Alma sank down beside her mother and hugged her. Hetty felt hot tears slide down her own cheeks.

CHAPTER 2
THE TENT RESTAURANT

Hetty sat on one side of Mrs. Vasquez, and Alma sat on the other, hugging her. Hetty looked at Papa. His beard was scraggly and wild. His green eyes had deep, smoky circles underneath. Hetty wondered if her own looked so empty and discouraged.

"We can't go home, Papa, we just can't. And we can't go on alone. I could never leave Alma behind."

"You're right, Hetty." Papa ran his fingers through his curly black hair. "You and Alma are like sisters, and Mrs. Vasquez has been a wonderful friend to our family. We all made the decision together to come. Whatever we decide to do, we're sticking together."

Mrs. Vasquez searched in the pocket of her voluminous red skirt until she found a handkerchief. She dried her eyes. Then she took a deep breath, squared her shoulders, and cleared her throat. "I'm too tired to think about this any more tonight. Things always look better in the morning."

Hetty didn't see how anything could improve overnight, unless Mrs. Vasquez found her money. They were quiet over dinner. Then they unpacked their blankets, rolled them out into beds, and got ready for their first night on Alaskan soil.

The next morning, while they were cooking breakfast, Colin Brandauer of the Northwest Mounted Police came by their tent. They had met the young Mountie on the steamer. He was one of twenty Mounties who were being sent into Alaska and Canada to help the Klondikers. Hetty wondered if he'd heard about someone taking Mrs. Vasquez's money.

"Good morning, Mrs. Vasquez, Hetty, Alma. Did you get off the steamer without mishap?" The Mountie stood tall and proud in his red coat, blue breeches with a stripe down each side, and shiny black boots.

"I'm afraid not," Mrs. Vasquez answered. "My purse disappeared. I've lost all my money."

Colin Brandauer shook his head. "That's a shame. Unfortunately, with all the confusion on the beach, theft is not uncommon. And there's not much law enforcement in Dyea. What do you plan to do? You need cash to make it through the winter in the Yukon." The Mountie looked at Mrs. Vasquez, then at Alma and Hetty. "This is a very difficult trip, and only the strongest and best-prepared people, the ones who can overcome adversity, are going to make it to Dawson."

"Are you saying we can't do it, Mr. Brandauer?" Hetty asked. "Make it to Dawson?"

"Please call me Colin, Hetty. You're the same age as my sister, and 'Mr. Brandauer' sounds like my father." He smiled at Hetty, then raised his eyebrows. "Are you a person who gives up easily?"

"I am not." What Hetty didn't say was, *Just let someone tell me I can't do something.* Her middle name was Stubborn.

"Overnight, I thought of a plan, Colin," Mrs. Vasquez said. "I'd be glad for your opinion on whether it will work. I see many hungry men out here without their wives to cook for them. I'm a very good cook. I thought I could set up a tent restaurant, cook our wet food, and charge for meals until I have enough for a grubstake."

Colin nodded. "I think that would work. You can buy new supplies from those who are already giving up—'icicle feet,' we call them."

Mrs. Vasquez smiled. "I brought some lumber along. I don't know what I was thinking—already I know I can't carry lumber up the mountain. Glen and I can build tables and benches for diners."

"You don't give up easily, Mrs. Vasquez. I admire that

in a person. I'll check on you again before I leave for the pass." Colin saluted Mrs. Vasquez, bowed to Hetty and Alma, and strolled away.

Hetty thought about the new plan while she ate breakfast. "Where's Papa, Mrs. V?" she asked.

"He said he was going to look for Donall. Your uncle didn't come home last night. We figure he found some all-night card game and is still there this morning. Why don't you girls go look for them both? I could use their help if I'm going to serve meals in a couple of days."

Hetty's Uncle Donall hadn't had the money to make the trek to the goldfields. But he'd begged Papa to let him come along anyway. Hetty hoped he wasn't off losing his share of the cash Papa had lent him. Papa was much more tolerant of his younger brother Donall's bad habits than Hetty was.

Hetty and Alma walked up and down the rows of tents. Most people were packing, getting ready to leave. All through the tent city, *hurry, hurry, hurry* was in the air. Everyone was in a hurry to get to the goldfields.

"Hetty, you've wanted to go home all along," Alma reminded her. "Mama losing her money was your chance. Are you disappointed that we're opening a restaurant instead of going home?"

"Well—" Hetty tried to imagine getting back on the boat where she had been seasick every day for a week. The steamer had been so crowded, there was hardly room to lie down. No one had gotten much sleep. “Now that we’ve come this far, I want to go on. Papa says we have to look every day for stories. What’s happened so far wouldn’t make a very good story.”

They took off toward the ocean and the buildings that made up the town of Dyea. The shortcut didn’t help them find Papa or Uncle Donall, but Hetty spotted Mr. Parker again. “I have an idea, Alma. Let’s go talk to him.”

Mr. Parker was sitting on a wooden box staring at the ocean that had robbed him of his dream. The fragrant smell of tobacco drifted from his pipe.

“Mr. Parker, Mr. Parker,” Hetty called to him. “We have an idea. Maybe you can go look for gold after all.”

Amos Parker stared at them for a moment, then came back from wherever his mind had been. “My goodness, I thought you two would be packing to leave on the trail tomorrow.”

“We can’t go yet,” Hetty said. She explained that Alma’s mother’s money was gone and that they planned to open a restaurant to earn it back. “We can cook up your wet food and sell it, too, so that you’d have money to buy supplies.”

Mr. Parker took another pull on his pipe and blew smoke at the swarm of mosquitoes buzzing around them. “I think I want to go home, girls. I’ve lost my heart for treasure seeking.”

After an hour of looking for Papa and Uncle Donall, Hetty and Alma got back to their camp to find Papa helping Mrs. Vasquez build some tables. Uncle Donall chose that moment to stroll up to the campfire. "Anything for me to do? Any coffee left?" he asked, testing the pot, then pouring a cup. He reached for some leftover bacon and rolled it in a tortilla for a sandwich.

Hetty was glad Papa spoke before she did. She didn't want to be disrespectful, but she was mad enough to forget she ever had any manners.

"Where have you been, Donall?" Papa asked. "We've needed help."

"I couldn't find you last night, and then I met the most fascinating couple. They're part of a Wild West show and—"

"You've been with *them*." Hetty's hands flew to her waist before she could stop them. "You've been off making new friends when your family needs you."

Uncle Donall smiled at Hetty. He had the same black, curly hair as Papa, but no beard. And his teasing eyes were the color of sweet violets in spring. "Oh, Hetty, we may need friends to help us climb the mountain. One can never have too many friends." He swiped at Hetty's chin. "Don't be mad at me, or we'll have to fight." He raised his fists and bounced around like a boxer.

Hetty sighed. It was hard to stay mad at Uncle Donall for long.

"I'm so glad to get off that ship, I could whip the best man in Alaska or California right now. I could fight off a grizzly bear with my bare hands." Uncle Donall punched the air.

"I'm going to be doing a lot of cooking. How about using that energy to find us firewood, Donall McKinley?" Mrs. Vasquez shook her big spoon at Uncle Donall. "If there's any left around here, with all these campfires."

Uncle Donall drank his last sip of coffee, smiled, and danced away. Hetty would be surprised if he came back with a load of wood.

"Come have lunch, girls, and then help me," Mrs. Vasquez said. "There's a lot to do if we're going to open the restaurant tomorrow." She had set up the camping stove and was stirring a big pot of beans.

The stove was only a sheet of iron balanced over the fire on small legs. Hetty couldn't believe they were going to cook their own meals on it, much less all the meals for a restaurant. But if the meal Mrs. Vasquez prepared that night was anything like what she'd serve in her restaurant, Hetty thought, they'd get rich in a week.

Mrs. Vasquez fried the tortillas that Alma and Hetty had helped her pat out, filled them with beans and spices, and rolled them up. Then she fried dried apples in butter, sugar, and cinnamon for a side dish. For dessert, they crunched puffy *sopaipillas,* squares of bread dough fried in lard, then rolled in sugar and cinnamon. Papa and Mrs.

Vasquez drank coffee while Alma and Hetty drank tinned milk, heated and flavored with cocoa powder and cinnamon.

At dusk, just as they were finishing dinner, Uncle Donall came back with an armload of wood and a young man about his age. They gobbled up a plateful of food, then disappeared again.

"It took him all afternoon to get wood. Now he's off to play cards, no doubt," Mrs. Vasquez commented, her voice scolding.

"Hetty and I will wash dishes, Mama. You go to bed." Alma and Hetty gathered the tin plates that were practically licked clean. "Maybe Uncle Donall and his friend will spread the news about your restaurant."

The news spread, all right. The next night, a line of people circled their tent. Hetty and Alma were too busy to count them, but Hetty was sure there were more than a hundred. Diners brought their own plates, cups, and silverware but paid a dollar to have the plate filled with tortillas and beans and the cup filled with coffee or tea.

Hetty and Alma had worked all day helping Mrs. Vasquez cook. By dinnertime, they were tired, but they'd put on their best dresses to help serve. Mrs. Vasquez had tied big white aprons over them. "No time to cook *and* do laundry," she'd said. Hetty had fingered her locket and made a wish that their restaurant plan would succeed.

The scene was one big party. When the tables were filled, people sat on the ground, laughing and talking as they ate. After dinner and a dessert of dried-apple pie, some customers stayed to sing or visit. A man played a fiddle, and a few couples danced.

Hetty was cleaning off a table when a boy walked up to her, a big grin on his face. It was the friendly boy from the beach, the one who had strolled past their campfire two nights ago. "My name is Eddie Jacobson. Is this your restaurant? Your ma sure can cook. Where are you from? We're from Oakland, California."

Hetty stared at Eddie, who was so full of talk. He had sandy hair, sparkling brown eyes, and the same teasing look that Uncle Donall always wore.

She was too tired to visit, but she tried to be polite. "My name is Hetty McKinley. Mrs. Vasquez is not my mother. She's my best friend Alma's mother. We're from San Francisco."

"Do you think we'll find gold nuggets the size of potatoes in the Yukon, like everyone says? How long are you staying in Dyea? Aren't you in a hurry to climb the mountain?" Eddie chattered on and on, not waiting for Hetty to answer his questions. She looked around, wishing Alma would come rescue her.

"Is my boy bothering you?" A tall, thin man walked up, an accordion strapped to his chest. "I'm William Jacobson.

We're neighbors." He pointed out his family. "That's my wife, Sophie, talking to Mrs. Vasquez. And that's our older son, Carl, and our baby girl, Rosie."

Hetty saw a woman with curly blond hair holding a chubby baby, whose red hair fell into ringlets all around her smiling face. Hetty recognized Carl as the sneering boy who had walked past their tent with Eddie that first evening in Dyea. Carl looked like his father—tall, slim, with dark hair and dark eyes—but he was the only one of the Jacobsons not smiling or laughing.

"Carl didn't want to come on this trip," Eddie said. "Play a jig, Pa. People want to dance."

Mr. Jacobson walked back to where the fiddler was tuning his violin. Soon the two played a lively duet that made Hetty want to dance, but her feet ached and there was still cleaning to do.

After the last customers had drifted away, and Mrs. Vasquez and Papa had gone to their tents, Hetty and Alma sat outside looking at the sky full of stars. Most of the camp was quiet, but here and there Hetty could hear laughter, a baby crying, and somewhere behind her, a flute playing a haunting melody. The air was crisp and clean and seemed lightweight compared to the air in San Francisco. Sounds carried from a distance. Hetty could even hear waves washing back and forth on the beach.

She decided to keep a list in her journal of all the ways Alaska and Canada were different from California, what she missed most from home, and what she liked best about this new place. Mama had taught her to see both sides of a picture, the good and the bad in a situation. It was good that they had gotten this far. It was bad that Mrs. Vasquez had lost her money—but look how many new people they were meeting by having a restaurant.

"What are you thinking, Alma?" Hetty asked.

"That this evening we may have waited on the man who took Mama's money."

"There are probably lots of thieves going to the goldfields." Hetty shivered. "Let's not think about that tonight."

They sat silently, almost too tired to talk but not wanting to go to bed. Hetty took off her locket and looked at the photo of her mother by the flickering light of the fire. Mama's face was so delicate, her eyes smiling and, even in the photo, mischievous. Hetty looked like Papa with her curly black hair and green eyes, her nearly square, no-nonsense face. Hetty sighed, closed the locket and put it back on, then slipped the heart under the collar of her dress.

She thought of Mrs. Vasquez, laughing and talking to people while she heaped their plates with food. She was just as efficient tonight in the restaurant as she had been running her store after her husband died. No anger or resentment was left about the reason she was working so hard. Mrs. Vasquez once said that the secret to being happy was to be like a rubber ball. When life throws you down, bounce back up.

"Your mother is wonderful, Alma. She truly bounces back when bad things happen."

"You miss your mother, don't you, Hetty?" Alma pulled her shawl tight around her shoulders. The two sat close together by the dying embers of the campfire.

"I will always miss her. She loved sitting on the porch at night, looking at the stars. But she could never have come on this trip. She was too frail. Papa and I would still be in California if she were alive. Mama was the one who taught me to write down my thoughts in my journal every night. Sometimes we read Miss Dickinson's poetry and I tried to make my thoughts into my own poem. Mama said my poems were wonderful, but I guess mothers always say that."

"You *are* a wonderful writer, Hetty." Alma stood up. "We'd better go to bed. We have to cook and feed people again tomorrow."

Both girls groaned loudly and then stifled their giggles as they slipped into the tent. Hetty would have liked to write in her journal, describe the restaurant and the new people they'd met, but it was all she could do to take off her dress, pull on her nightgown, and crawl under her blankets.

The next night, Hetty again had no time to think about poetry and no energy to write in her journal. She barely had time to think. It seemed that double the number of people showed up for dinner. Only when food ran out did she and Alma have time to sit at a table and eat their own meal.

"Look at that man over there, Hetty," Alma whispered as she took a bite of beans. "His face is all mashed in."

Hetty saw who Alma was talking about. She remembered serving him earlier. His face was crooked, his chin off to one side. But he was laughing and talking, and she had noticed his sparkling blue eyes.

"He must have been in some terrible accident," Hetty whispered back. She hadn't spoken softly enough, though.

"That's Andy Nickerson," a deep voice behind her said. "But everyone calls him Moosejaw. Want to hear how his face got smashed?"

Hetty was surprised when a stocky young man eased onto the bench across from her. Papa sat down next to him.

"Here's someone I'm sure you'll enjoy meeting, Hetty," Papa said, sipping his coffee. "He's a writer. His name is Jack London. Jack, meet my daughter, Hetty, who wants to be a writer, and her friend Alma. Alma's mother runs this excellent restaurant."

"As fine a place to eat as any in California or Alaska." Jack stuck out his hand to Hetty and then to Alma. His grip was firm, and his hand, which swallowed Hetty's, was rough with calluses. Hetty thought that perhaps he had done harder work in his life than writing.

"Jack won a contest at the *San Francisco Call* four years ago," Papa said. "We paid him twenty-five dollars, if I remember right."

Jack laughed. "Yes, money I needed badly. I had just returned from working on a seal-hunting expedition in Siberia with more stories than cash."

"I will never forget your descriptions of slaughtering the seals onboard your ship," Papa said.

"I can never forget those awful scenes. I found myself trapped in a sea of blood for a hundred days in order to provide women with fur coats."

Hetty shivered and vowed never to wear a sealskin coat. "Are you truly a writer? I've never met a writer before, except, of course, for Papa, who's a journalist." Hetty knew she sounded like a silly schoolgirl, but how exciting this was! "Papa said I must come on this trip so I'd have an adventure. Have you published stories in magazines?"

"Young lady, I have the tallest stack of rejection slips in California." Jack threw back his head and laughed.

Jack's hair was as yellow as a hay field and his eyes as blue as the sea on a summer day. He was short, not a lot taller than Hetty, but his shoulders were broad, his body strong. His eyes studied her, but he looked as though he waited for her to say something fascinating.

She could only stare. Papa saved her. "I told Hetty she had to come on this trip so she'd have new things to write about."

"Your father is right. I plan to write no fewer than a thousand words a day while in Alaska." Jack stared at the last *sopaipilla* on Alma's plate. Alma giggled and offered it to him. He smiled and popped it into his mouth.

"A thousand words?" Hetty asked. "Goodness, I'm way behind already. What do you write about?"

"The characters I meet. The scenery. The frightened horses being unloaded from the ship onto the beach. The thousands of people hoping to strike it rich." Jack licked sugar from his short, stubby fingers.

"You were going to tell us how that poor man got his face mashed," Alma reminded Jack.

"Ah, yes, Moosejaw. The winters are long and cold in the Yukon. Moosejaw has been prospecting near Dawson for several years. Men, living in one-room cabins, get lonely. They do strange things. Mr. Nickerson brought a young moose into his cabin for company."

"Right into his house?" Alma giggled again. "Like a puppy?"

"That's right. But one day, when they went outside together, Mother Moose found her baby and repaid Nickerson for baby-sitting by kicking him in the face."

"You're teasing us." Hetty thought Jack was telling tall tales.

"Ask him. He tells the story to anyone who'll listen. You'll find many men with strange nicknames living in the goldfields."

"Are you seeking gold, Jack?" Papa asked.

"I am seeking adventure. If gold appears under my fingers, however, I will certainly pick it up." Jack London stood. "Are you leaving tomorrow?"

"We can't leave until we earn a little more money." Papa didn't bother Jack with the details of being robbed.

"Well, good luck. We'll meet again, I hope. And when we do, Hetty, we will share stories. You read me yours. I'll read you mine."

Hetty watched Jack London walk away. Jack wasn't very old, but look at the experiences he'd had, the places he'd been! She had never traveled anywhere until now. How could she share what she wrote with him? The idea was much too frightening. But she vowed to write in her journal every night as he advised. Papa was right. She needed this adventure.

CHAPTER 3
SARAH LANCASTER

After a week of hard work, Hetty woke up sore and tired. She stretched and snuggled under her blankets, thinking that she'd rather climb the world's tallest mountain than keep on dishing up food for hungry people and cleaning up afterward. But today was their last day in Dyea. Their restaurant had been so successful that they had raised enough money to pay for Mrs. Vasquez's share of the trip and to replace Papa's soaked food.

Meeting new people every night had been fun. Mrs. Vasquez had gotten three marriage proposals, but each time she had only laughed and said, "No thanks." There was always music and dancing. Papa had brought a copy of *Great Expectations* by Mr. Charles Dickens. Some nights he read a chapter aloud, and many diners stayed to listen.

Tomorrow, they would start their trip up the trail

toward Chilkoot Pass. Most of the people they'd arrived with on the steamer had already left. New boats arrived every day, bringing new people eager to head for the gold-fields. Every night Hetty saw new faces at their restaurant.

Jack London had left. Colin Brandauer was gone. But Andy Nickerson—Moosejaw—was still here, coming over every night. Hetty wondered if he was interested in more than Mrs. Vasquez's good cooking.

The Jacobsons were still camped nearby, too. Papa and William Jacobson had become best friends. Eddie said the reason they hadn't left for the pass was that his mother had been ill and needed to rest. Eddie came to visit every day, often bringing Rosie, with her curly red hair and giggles. Hetty and Alma got to be friends with Eddie, and they loved playing with the sweet, laughing baby. They hardly ever saw Carl, and when they did, he was never friendly.

Hetty stretched her sore muscles and stopped daydreaming. Realizing that it was late and she was probably the last one in bed, she rushed to dress, slip on her locket, and pull a shawl around her shoulders.

She stepped outside the tent and took a deep breath. The morning was foggy and the air smelled of campfire smoke. A few snowflakes floated down. San Francisco had had a freak snowfall in '96, but other than that, Hetty had never experienced snow. She was eager for their first real Alaskan snowfall.

"Good morning, sleepyhead," Mrs. Vasquez said. She sat on a folded blanket near the campfire, patting lumps of dough into tortillas.

Alma sat beside her mother, helping. "We decided since this is our last day, we'd let you out of some of the work. Wasn't that kind of us?" Alma's dark hair was perfectly braided, and her brown eyes sparkled. Hetty couldn't see a spot of mud on her dress.

Hetty hadn't looked in a mirror, but she could see wisps of her own curly hair all around her face. She was trying to keep it braided so it would stay out of the way, but her hair had a mind of its own.

"Thank you for all your hard work this week, Hetty," Mrs. Vasquez said. "I'll wash your dress today. Wear another that's clean."

"I can wash it, Mrs. V," Hetty offered, but she dreaded trying to wash clothes in a tub of water outside the tent.

A sudden cold wind made her tug her shawl closer. It was time to find her winter coat and September was just ending. Someone had told her that the winters in Dawson could be fifty to seventy degrees below zero. She couldn't imagine such frigid temperatures.

"Where are Papa and Uncle Donall?" Hetty dished up a bowl of oatmeal, adding a splash of tinned milk and a spoonful of their precious sugar.

"They went to gather firewood," Mrs. V said. "But let me guess. Your papa has gotten distracted talking to people, looking for good stories. And Donall discovered a card game or a lady to flirt with."

Hetty didn't disagree. Mrs. Vasquez knew both men well. Why had Hetty bothered to ask where they were?

As Hetty finished breakfast, Uncle Donall put in an appearance. But he wasn't alone. On his arm was a very pretty woman wearing a big picture hat covered with pink tulle roses and artificial violets.

"Maria Vasquez, Alma, and Hetty, I want you to meet my new friend. This is Sarah Lancaster. She's also from San Francisco—not that working folks like us would have met her before. I believe she lives on Nob Hill. She came this far all alone, but she needs a group to team up with. So I've invited Sarah to travel with us."

Hetty was speechless. Uncle Donall had asked someone to join them without first getting Papa and Mrs. V's permission? A woman who looked as if she was going to a tea party. Someone who was probably used to having maids to wait on her every minute of every day. Hetty was sure Sarah Lancaster would be totally helpless camping out and climbing a mountain.

Why, look at her! Besides the impractical hat, Sarah Lancaster was dressed in a fashionable navy-blue suit with a skirt that came to her ankles.

"I'm so pleased to meet all of you," Sarah Lancaster said, her face all smiles. "Aren't you just too-too excited about this adventure? Oh, I can hardly wait to get started.

But I told Donall that, although I had come this far alone, I could never climb the mountain alone. Oh, I have plenty of supplies." She put out her hand to stop any protests. "I plan to carry my goods myself or hire Indian packers. But I would be too-too lonely spending all my time by myself. I'll pay my share, you should know that. I have plenty of money. But an adventure like this should be shared."

Sarah Lancaster looked at Uncle Donall and smiled a huge smile. "Don't you think so?"

Obviously Uncle Donall thought they should share their trip with Sarah Lancaster, but Hetty couldn't imagine doing so. And by the look on Alma's and Mrs. V's faces, Hetty could tell they agreed with her.

"I think we should ask Papa, don't you, Uncle Donall?" Hetty stared at him, sending him all sorts of messages that she couldn't begin to put into words in front of Sarah Lancaster.

Papa walked up in time to hear what Hetty said. "Ask me what, Hetty? And who is this charming lady?"

Uncle Donall made introductions again, and Papa took Sarah Lancaster's hand. "I'm so pleased to meet you. I see no reason why you can't join us. The more the—"

"Papa, may I talk to you?" Hetty asked.

"Oh, please, could you talk to your papa later, Hetty?" Sarah interrupted, breathless. "One reason I came over to your tent, besides wanting to meet you so badly, is that I found a photographer on the beach. For a dollar he'll take our picture. Don't you want a picture at the start of our adventure? I do. Please come with me, you and Alma both."

Sarah put out her white-gloved hand and wouldn't take it back until Hetty put hers in it. Hetty looked at Alma.

Alma raised her shoulders slightly and widened her eyes. "May I go, Mama?"

"I think a picture at the beginning of our trip would be a nice memento for your scrapbook, but I need you right back to help with tonight's food." Mrs. Vasquez hesitated, then searched in her pocket.

"Oh, my treat, Mrs. Vasquez. The photos are my treat." Sarah waved at Alma's mother and tugged Hetty away from the fire. She hooked her other arm into the crook of Uncle Donall's and swept them away toward the beach. Snowflakes stopped and the sun tried to come out, as if reflecting Sarah's mood.

They wove their way through tents toward the rush of the ocean, the screaming gulls, and the eager voices of new people arriving.

Just ahead, up on the beach, away from where the tide could come in and take his props, Hetty saw a man with a big, black-draped camera.

"Take your photo, sir? Take your photo, ma'am?" he asked.

The man led Sarah and Uncle Donall to a little stage with a painted background of a rickety wooden shack.

He offered Uncle Donall his choice of a goldpan, an axe, or a rifle, and then he handed Sarah a bouquet of wildflowers.

Sarah Lancaster clutched the flowers and tugged Uncle Donall close to her, pushing a goldpan into his hands. Uncle Donall tried to strike a serious pose, but Sarah Lancaster tilted her head and laughed.

Many people stopped to watch, then stood in line to be next.

"They look like a bride and groom," Alma whispered to Hetty.

"Please, Alma, please don't say such a thing," Hetty whispered back, though she had to admit that Uncle Donall, with his unruly curling hair and his big smile, and Sarah Lancaster, with her sparkling green eyes, made a handsome couple. Sarah was almost as tall as Uncle Donall and as thin as a willow tree. She reminded Hetty of a spirited horse, ready to gallop off at the slightest impulse.

Once the first photo was taken, Sarah pushed Uncle Donall away and tugged Hetty and Alma in front of the camera. "Girls only," she said, laughing again. She hugged Hetty close as if she had known her for years. Hetty tried to smile at the photographer as he stepped back under the cloth draping his camera, but she found she could scarcely breathe.

"Come back in four hours for your photographs,"

the photographer said, taking Sarah Lancaster's money.

They watched the next man pose for his picture. Suddenly a gust of wind blew over the painted background and nearly took Sarah's big hat. Sarah grabbed it and placed it back on her head, tilting it to a flirty angle. Alma asked the question that had formed in Hetty's mind, too.

"Are you planning to wear that hat on the trail, Miss Lancaster?"

"Oh, yes, Alma. My friends in San Francisco made me a bet that I couldn't wear a stylish hat all the way to Dawson. I can never resist a bet, can you, Alma?"

A bet? A bet! Uncle Donall's favorite word. No wonder he was attracted to this woman. They were two of a kind.

Hetty stared at Uncle Donall and Sarah Lancaster as they lingered near the beach, chatting and waving at new friends. She and Alma, Papa and Mrs. Vasquez were going to climb to the top of a snow-covered pass with this butterfly of a woman?

Hetty took a deep breath, bit her bottom lip to hold back a sob, and then thought, *At least she's wearing sensible shoes.*

CHAPTER 4
ON THE TRAIL

The next morning they got up at first light and dressed quickly in the frosty air. Hetty's stomach was so jumpy, she could eat only a few bites of her cold breakfast. Once Papa and Uncle Donall took the tents down, Hetty stared at the huge piles of supplies, some stacks six feet high. The stacks included Sarah Lancaster's provisions, which Sarah, Uncle Donall, and Papa had moved over last night after dinner.

Those who could afford to hire Native packers could get to Chilkoot Pass in a few days. But Papa and Uncle Donall had figured out that, if they had good luck, it would take them a month. Hetty had hoped Sarah Lancaster would decide to go on without them once she heard that, but she seemed determined to stay with Uncle Donall.

Hetty glanced around to see Sarah hurrying into camp

pushing a two-wheeled cart. "A man in Dyea is selling these. I just couldn't see carrying all my supplies on my back if I could use a cart to haul them. A boy is coming right behind me with another cart, Maria. I bought you one, too. Now, don't protest." Sarah held out her hand to Mrs. Vasquez, and Hetty noticed that she had exchanged her white gloves for brown leather ones. "We can't afford to have our chief cook too tired at night, can we?"

Mrs. Vasquez looked at Sarah and shrugged, and together they set to work. They tied down a huge load, maybe three hundred pounds, on each cart. Hetty could easily see that the carts, whose wheels were almost as high as Hetty was tall, would save time and energy.

Sarah showed Mrs. Vasquez what she'd learned about handling the carts. "Coming over here, I tried pushing and pulling. I definitely think pushing is easier, as long as you look out for rocks on the trail."

Uncle Donall brought Hetty and Alma the first of their loads. Each pack weighed about twenty pounds.

"I'm not sure I can carry twenty pounds." Hetty lifted her pack, groaned, then grinned at Uncle Donall.

"The load will feel lighter when it's on your back. And you have no choice, Sissy Girl." Uncle Donall knew the right words to use to get Hetty angry enough to lift anything.

While they waited for Papa to finish organizing the provisions, Mrs. V pulled Hetty and Alma behind her cart and showed them where she had hidden her money. Half was in the bottom of her small trunk and half in a specially marked bag of rice. "I don't plan to be robbed again," Mrs. V said. "But if anything happens to me, I want you two girls to know where my money is."

"Nothing is going to happen to you, Mama," Alma said, looking worried.

"You never know. This is going to be a very difficult trip."

When they seemed ready to leave, Papa called everyone together to discuss plans for the day.

"Finnegans Point is the place where most Klondikers camp after leaving Dyea. But that's four miles away, and I figure we can't haul all our supplies that far in a day. So we'll take our first loads to the halfway point and set up camp. One of us will stay there to guard our belongings while the rest come back for more loads. I've asked Donall to stand guard on this end until the last load is moved. We need a strong person to guard in Dyea, since the risk of theft seems greater here."

"I'm willing to stand guard here," Uncle Donall said, leaning on a pile of goods and lighting his pipe, "if Maria stands guard at the new camp."

"And perhaps starts supper?" Mrs. V said, smiling at Donall.

"That, too." Uncle Donall returned one of his own charming smiles.

"Are we ready for the big adventure at last?" Papa asked, looking at his pocket watch and hoisting his pack.

"Ready!" everyone shouted. "Let's go!"

Hetty, Alma, and Papa shouldered their packs and followed Mrs. V and Sarah, pushing carts, through the tent city toward the trail.

Andy Nickerson waved at Mrs. V as they passed his camp. "See you at Finnegans Point."

Eddie Jacobson ran to catch up to Hetty and Alma. "We're leaving in a few minutes. We'll look for you tonight, or at Finnegans Point."

Thousands of Klondikers were already moving along the trail toward Chilkoot Pass. Until the trail widened, Hetty and Alma had to walk quickly, or people behind them grumbled or bumped into them. Everyone was excited and acted as if they could reach the pass today.

They couldn't see Chilkoot Pass, but several snow-covered peaks, backed by a rare blue sky, looked millions of miles away. Hetty couldn't imagine walking that far.

"Look at those mountains, Hetty," Papa said, walking beside her. "Have you ever seen anything so awe-inspiring? Don't you wish your mother was here to see such a sight?"

How like Papa, Hetty thought, to notice every detail of their surroundings. And to think of Mama now, just the way he shared everything with her when she was alive.

The trail was level and soon widened so that people could spread out. Hetty and Alma, who were following

Mrs. V's and Sarah's carts, could slow down. The Dyea River rushed along on the west side of the trail, and on the other side they passed groves of cottonwood and birch, the leaves turning yellow after fall frosts. Dark green spruce trees and red bushlike thickets made a lovely contrast of color. When Hetty listened carefully, she could hear the *chip, chip, chip* of sparrows in the brush. A crow rose from a cottonwood branch, croaking in a hoarse voice—no doubt wondering, Hetty thought, why so many people had come to disturb his home.

The trail was fairly smooth, but even so, Hetty was glad she had good, sturdy, ankle-high shoes. They weren't pretty, but she knew she was going to walk more on this trip than she had ever walked in her life.

Before they'd gone a half-mile, Hetty's pack rubbed her shoulders and felt unwieldy. She bent over and tried to balance it better. "I think we got the wrong packs," she said to Alma. "These must weigh a hundred pounds."

Alma giggled because Hetty was exaggerating again. "Are you scared about climbing this mountain, Hetty?" she asked, taking Hetty's hand.

"Yes," Hetty admitted. "I've been scared ever since we left home, but I've told myself it's okay. Scared and excited and eager sometimes get all mixed up in my head. But maybe if I had a big picture hat, I'd think I could do anything." Hetty and Alma laughed. Laughing helped. Hetty vowed to do a lot of laughing.

"I'm scared that I can't keep up, carrying this pack," Alma said.

"Try not to think about the load you're carrying."

Alma sighed and shifted her backpack. "What else is there to think about?"

"The scenery. And all these trunks and boxes piled along the path. Have you noticed that no one is guarding them? Don't you wonder what's in them?" Hetty's imagination filled in the answers to all the questions that flew through her mind.

"I wish I were a writer," Alma said. "You're so lucky to be able to write stories and poetry, Hetty. When we come back rich, and you're a famous lady writer, you can step right into high society, right on Nob Hill. You can dress like Sarah Lancaster."

"By then, Alma, you and your mother will have found a fortune in gold, settled on Nob Hill yourself, and opened a famous restaurant with crystal chandeliers. I'll bring all my writer friends to eat there every night."

They lost sight of Sarah, but as they walked at a steady pace, following Mrs. V to help her if her cart got stuck, Hetty daydreamed about all the things she'd do once she and Papa found gold.

It was late morning when they came upon Sarah Lancaster, resting beside the trail, reading a book of poetry. "There you are," she said.

"Did you bring that book of poetry with you from

San Francisco?" Hetty asked. "Books are so heavy, Papa would let me bring only two."

"No, I found it." Sarah pointed to a trunk and some wooden crates right behind her.

"But aren't the owners coming back?" Hetty asked.

"I saw a woman abandon this trunk. She was crying, but she said she realized she'd brought too much. Let's look in it. I only took out this book." Sarah jumped up, lifted the lid, and unpacked more as Hetty, Alma, and Mrs. V watched.

"Nothing worthwhile," Sarah said, as she set aside a lamp and a strangely shaped vase.

"Don't you feel funny rummaging through someone else's private life?" Hetty finally asked.

"It's just stuff." Sarah held up some pink beads and earrings to match. "Look, this jewelry is cheap glass."

"It wasn't just stuff to whoever packed it," Mrs. Vasquez said. "It meant something to them, or they wouldn't have brought it along."

"Maybe the woman's husband gave her those beads on their first wedding anniversary. Or her birthday," Hetty added, thinking of how Papa had given her mother gifts on every occasion.

Sarah looked at Hetty for a long moment. She placed everything back in the trunk and shut the lid. "You have a wonderful imagination, Hetty," she said. "I'm eager to get to know you better."

"Should we have a bite of lunch even though it's early?" Mrs. V asked. "I was too excited to eat breakfast."

Sarah helped Mrs. V set out some cold bacon and tortillas, along with a handful of dried peaches each. "I'm going to build a tiny fire," Sarah said. "A cup of tea will make us all feel wonderful for the afternoon's walk."

"She makes the trail seem like a stroll in the park, doesn't she, Hetty?" Alma whispered. "Maybe when we get to know her—"

"Maybe." Hetty stopped Alma from saying that they'd like Sarah Lancaster better.

A light rain started to fall that afternoon and worsened the next day. With the wet weather, it took them three days, even longer than they'd thought, to get to Finnegans Point. Each night, they'd been almost too tired to set up their tents, eat, and crawl into bed. "We'll get used to it," Uncle Donall had said, but instead of agreement, he got groans in response.

By the time they'd hauled everything to Finnegans Point, they were so tired and sore that Uncle Donall and Papa decided they ought to rest for a couple of days. All of them realized that they weren't going to get to Chilkoot Pass quickly, maybe not even in a month. Papa admitted he hadn't carried more than a notebook for years, and although Uncle Donall didn't say so, Hetty figured he hadn't carried more than a pack of cards.

Hetty and Alma helped Mrs. V set up camp, and then Mrs. V sent them to look for firewood. Trees surrounded the tent city of Finnegans Point, but all the dead logs and branches had been cut and gathered.

"We're going to have to walk farther into the woods," Alma said, "and none of the wood we find will be dry."

"I just want to lie down and sleep for a couple of days," Hetty said, groaning, "but I guess if we want supper, we'd better find some firewood."

Clouds lowered and it got dark and cold, but after a good dinner, everyone felt better. Several people stopped to see if Mrs. Vasquez was selling meals. "Not this time," she answered with a smile.

"Ah, the beautiful lady cook." Andy Nickerson showed up, carrying his own tin cup of tea, looking for company—maybe only the company of Mrs. Vasquez. Moosejaw said that "by luck" he had camped nearby.

"Let's go look around the town," Hetty whispered to Alma, not knowing if Mrs. V would tell them it wasn't safe to do so. Hetty hoped Mrs. V would be distracted enough not to notice if they left.

"I'll go with you," Sarah Lancaster whispered. She jumped up, a shawl tied over her hat to keep it dry, another pulled tight around her shoulders. "Donnie has slipped off without me. Maybe I'll find him if we look around."

Donnie? Hetty realized that she meant Uncle Donall. She had never heard anyone call him that, and she felt a smile creep over her face as Sarah said it.

Hetty would rather have gone alone with Alma, but the three set off toward the twenty or so permanent tents and buildings that made up the town.

"Look, there are the Jacobsons," Alma said. "I wonder if they got here before we did."

Alma and Hetty waved at the family, who were still eating supper around their campfire. Eddie jumped up, but his mother pushed him back down. Maybe he'd come find them later.

Near the edge of town, they came across a woman, hands on her hips, staring at an enormous pile of barrels and crates. "That snake. That low-bellied snake!" the woman swore.

"What's the matter?" Sarah Lancaster asked.

"The matter is that I hired a man to take my things over the pass to Lake Lindeman, where I had a boat waiting to ferry them to Dawson. Now I find them dumped and abandoned here." She pressed her lips into a thin line. "I paid that swindler four thousand dollars. He took my money but apparently had no intention of doing the job."

"What's in all these crates?" asked Sarah.

"Fine linens, curtains and bedding, crystal glasses and china dishes. I plan to build a hotel in Dawson." The woman muttered as she looked into a trunk that was open.

Then she turned back to them and held out her hand. “I’m sorry, this is none of your fault. I’m Belinda Mulrooney.”

Hetty saw that Miss Mulrooney was well dressed in a riding skirt and boots, a warm jacket with a sheepskin collar, leather gloves, and a wool hat. Her face held a look of determination that set her apart from most women Hetty had seen on the trip.

“By heavens, I won’t be swindled! I’m going to find that no-good packer and get my money back! Would you mind watching my things while I go into town and find a reliable person to guard my belongings for a day or two?”

“We’d be glad to,” Hetty said. They watched the woman stomp off toward the restaurant and saloon.

“I want to see what she’s brought,” Sarah said the minute Belinda Mulrooney disappeared.

“I don’t think we should.” Hetty was curious, too, but she felt they should ask Miss Mulrooney first.

Sarah ignored Hetty. “Won’t hurt. We’re doing her a favor. Come on.”

Sarah led them to the open trunk. Inside were stacks of crisp white linen tablecloths and napkins. In a corner of each napkin, someone had embroidered a very fancy *M*. Despite herself, Hetty ran her fingers over the satiny embroidery. She watched Sarah Lancaster look to see if any other crate had broken open. Maybe Sarah was just a very curious person, Hetty thought. She let curiosity take first place over privacy.

"I'm going to find Donall," Sarah said suddenly. "Are you two afraid to stay here by yourself?"

"Of course not," Hetty answered. She sat on a big rock beside Alma.

Darkness surrounded them and a thick, cottony fog crept in. Music from the small tent town drifted back to where the girls sat. Wood smoke filled the night air. Occasionally they heard someone laughing or calling out to another.

When Miss Mulrooney returned, she thanked them and invited them to stay at her hotel when she got it finished.

"We will. Good luck." Hetty and Alma ran back to their camp. Mr. Jacobson and Papa sat by the fire discussing a book they'd both read before they left California. Ordinarily, Hetty would have stopped to listen, but tonight she ducked into her tent, since she wanted to write in her journal.

Mrs. V was already bundled into her blankets and asleep when Hetty and Alma slipped in. In the dark, Hetty hurried to undress, then pulled her flannel nightgown over her long underwear. She took off her locket and placed it beside her bedroll. Finally, she lit a candle, took out her journal, and began to write.

So far I have met two women who are making this trip alone. Never would I have thought that possible. I'm not sure I like Sarah Lancaster, but look how independent she is. I'm beginning to think she joined us only because she likes Uncle Donall. She didn't need us at all. She just wanted to spend more time with him.

Belinda Mulrooney is the most determined woman I have ever met. She is starting a hotel in Dawson by herself! And what did she decide to do when someone robbed and cheated her? She is going to take off on her horse and find him!

Hetty smiled in the dark. Belinda Mulrooney's determination had rubbed off on her. She hoped that, after a good night's sleep, they'd get back on the trail, too. She fingered her pencil a moment, then added a few last lines.

Now I'm going to write something that is too strange to tell anyone, even Alma. Inside, way deep inside, I feel a tiny fire growing bigger and bigger, as if the flame is being fed by meeting these determined women. I can climb this mountain. I can be a writer. I believe I can do anything I want to do.

Hetty closed her journal and laid her pencil and locket on top of it. She was almost too excited to sleep, but finally she drifted off.

The next morning, she was awakened by the sounds of dogs barking, people shouting to each other, someone chopping wood. She sat up, wide awake. The tent was dim and shadowy. Sarah and Alma were still asleep, but Mrs. V's bed was empty. Hetty reached for her pencil, a new thought in her head. Holding the pencil in her mouth, she felt for her locket.

Her locket! Frantically she searched under her journal, in her blankets, around her heap of clothing. Her locket was gone!

Chapter 5
More Is Missing

As Hetty got dressed, she shook her clothes and searched the folds of her blanket. She couldn't lose her picture of Mama! She bit her lip and held back tears. Tears never helped. She'd find the locket. She had had it last night. It must be here someplace. No one would steal it. It wasn't worth a lot of money, and besides, a thief would have had to sneak into their tent last night to take it, risk waking them all. It didn't make sense.

Hetty glanced at the sleeping Sarah and a memory surfaced. *It's just stuff*—that was Sarah's attitude toward trinkets like her locket. But the picture of her mother wasn't just stuff!

Hetty grabbed one of her blankets, wrapped it around her like a shawl, and stepped out of the tent. The sky was just getting light.

Mrs. Vasquez had a fire going, but she hadn't started

breakfast. She sat, huddled and wrapped in her own blanket, her hands around a cup of tea. Hetty sat down close beside her.

"Have you seen my locket, Mrs. V? I can't find it anywhere." Hetty touched the hollow of her neck where the silver heart had always hung.

"I haven't, Hetty." Mrs. V filled Hetty's cup full of steaming tea, then placed her arm around Hetty's shoulders and hugged her close. "I was going to ask you if you'd seen my brooch. Maybe I was foolish to wear it on the trail, but my husband gave it to me, and I've been missing him. It was just a glass gewgaw, but I liked it."

"Do you—do you think someone could have taken them? It's too much of a coincidence to think we both lost jewelry at the same time." Hetty pulled her blanket tighter against the cold.

Mrs. V started to cry softly. "Oh, Hetty, it's not just jewelry that's missing. Half my money is gone, the half I had hidden in the rice bag."

Hetty tried to take in what Mrs. V was saying, but the news only got worse.

"I can't go on, Hetty. I can't earn another five hundred dollars. Alma and I are going to turn back."

"But—Alma—I can't go on without Alma. We've been best friends forever. And I—I can't leave you." To her dismay, Hetty started to cry. She set down the cup of tea and sobbed into her wadded-up blanket.

When she finally got control, she wiped her eyes, took a sip of tea, and looked up to see Papa and Uncle Donall walking from their tent toward the fire. Papa buttoned his big coat and Uncle Donall blew on his hands and rubbed them together.

"Hetty, sweetheart, why are you crying? Is it too cold for you?" Uncle Donall asked. "Here, snuggle by me and get warm." He sat down by Hetty and hugged her. Somehow his concern made things just that much worse.

"Mrs. Vasquez—Alma—they're not going any farther." Hetty sobbed out the news.

"Maria?" Papa asked. "You're giving up? That's not like you. What's wrong?"

Mrs. Vasquez sighed and rubbed her eyes. "I'm a fool, Glen. Someone has robbed me again. Half the money I made at the tent restaurant in Dyea is gone."

Hetty still couldn't believe it. "You hid it so well, Mrs. V. I saw you hide it. How could someone find it in the—"

"I don't know, Hetty."

"Was there any time last night when we were all gone, when a thief could have come into the tent?" Hetty asked.

Uncle Donall finished his cup of coffee, hugged Hetty again, and stood up. "Maybe you're mistaken, Maria. Look again. I'm sure you'll find it." He ran his hands through his curly hair to comb it and walked away from them toward the restaurant and saloon.

Hetty watched him go. Uncle Donall was acting strange.

An idea ran through her mind before she could stop it. Could he have taken Mrs. Vasquez's money?

Before her mother had died, she had taught Hetty about handling the family's money. "Your papa can't manage money, Hetty. You're going to have to do it when I'm gone. And be careful of your Uncle Donall. He has a way of charming money out of your papa and sometimes even me. He's a sweet, dear man, but he's irresponsible. Your papa has spoiled him since he was a little boy."

Occasionally Uncle Donall *had* charmed Hetty out of money. He always promised to pay it back. Sometimes he did, but more often he forgot. Once she had noticed a few dollars missing from her hiding place, but several days later, just when she was set to accuse him of stealing, he came dancing into the house with a bouquet of flowers, a bag of her favorite hard candy, and the money he'd "borrowed." The cards had gone his way the night before.

"Papa." Hetty kept her voice low while Mrs. Vasquez started breakfast. "You know how easy it is to find a card game. Do you think Uncle Donall—"

"Of course not, Hetty. I'll not have you thinking that." Papa turned to Mrs. Vasquez. "Maria, I believe I have enough money for us all. Please continue on with us. We need you and Alma on this trip."

Papa patted his waist. "I'm wearing all of my money, Maria. Maybe that's what you should do from now on."

Sarah Lancaster stepped out of the tent, sticking a pin

in her big hat. True to her wager, she hadn't taken off her hat except to sleep. "What are you talking about so early in the morning? Is that tea, Mrs. Vasquez? Could I trouble you for a cup? Maybe it will help me wake up. Goodness, Donnie and I were playing cards till so late last night. I'm afraid Donnie was losing most of the evening, but I did rather well." Sarah looked around. "Where is Donnie? Is he still asleep?"

"He already left. He was heading toward town." Hetty couldn't believe that Sarah Lancaster had been out playing cards and gambling with Uncle Donall. Mama had always said such behavior was unladylike, but maybe the ladies on Nob Hill thought otherwise.

"I'm going to find him." Sarah jumped up. "I'll have breakfast in town, Mrs. Vasquez. Don't go to any trouble for me or Donnie."

"It's hard to dislike that woman," Mrs. Vasquez said, as soon as Sarah Lancaster was gone. "She and Donall make a handsome pair, don't they?"

Hetty had to admit that they did, but somehow both of them worried her. Without thinking, Hetty reached up to rub her locket. Then she remembered it was gone. Somehow not having it around her neck made her feel as though she'd lost her mother all over again.

Later that morning, with the sun trying to burn through a foggy haze, Mrs. Vasquez told Papa she'd take him up on his offer to help her. But she promised to pay him back once they found gold.

At dinner that night, Papa and Mr. Jacobson decided they could make better time if they all teamed up together. Sarah had heard the trail got steeper, so she and Mrs. V sold their carts to people who were giving up, returning to Dyea. Now all of them would have to carry backpacks with heavy loads.

Andy Nickerson said he'd go on to Pleasant Camp, the next stopping place, and save some good camping sites. He didn't have as much to carry, since he'd left most of his things in Dawson and had come to Dyea only to replenish his food. Hetty knew he could have been across the pass already, but he seemed to be looking after them.

Back on the trail the next morning, Alma and Hetty walked slowly side by side, with people bumping and jostling as they hurried around them. Hetty watched them but hardly saw individuals, her mind still puzzling over who could have taken the money and jewelry. She told Alma that she suspected Uncle Donall had taken the money, but he surely wouldn't have taken her locket with Mama's picture.

"I think Eddie Jacobson took your locket," Alma said. "He told us his mother's birthday was coming up. And you heard him mention that she always wanted a necklace like that. He could have slipped into our tent at night. They were camping near us. Maybe he took the money, too."

"I remember Eddie admiring my locket. I thought it was strange for a boy to notice jewelry." Hetty chewed on her lip. "But I like Eddie. I hate to think he'd steal from us. Besides, it wouldn't make sense for Eddie to give my locket to his mother for a birthday present. As soon as she saw it, she'd recognize it as mine."

"I hadn't thought of that. I guess you're right, but still, we should keep an eye on Eddie. We don't know him very well."

They stopped to rest, since Papa had warned them that the hardest climb of the morning was coming up. Hetty shifted and adjusted her pack, trying to get comfortable—if that was possible.

The Dyea River had cut a deep bed through the sand and gravel. On both sides of the narrow river valley, snow had melted, then turned to ice. Rock, encased in ice, rose up all around them. The trees seemed taller than any they had seen.

They made such slow progress—carrying, stopping, carrying, stopping—that Hetty wondered if they'd ever reach tonight's campsite. Cold rain kept falling. Everything was wet, and everyone was wet and cold and tired, so Hetty kept her misery to herself. She couldn't help but think that nothing had felt right since her locket disappeared.

Rain turned to snow. A coating of white covered rocks

and driftwood, making it hard to know where to step. Picking out each place to put her foot made for slow, miserable progress. Once Hetty fell when her foot slid off a rock. She couldn't get up until she tugged off her heavy backpack. Alma helped her put it back on. Hetty was so tired, she fought to keep back tears, but she and Alma kept going.

"Look, Hetty, the sun is coming out at last," Alma said. "And see, up ahead, Mama and the others have stopped for lunch. Mrs. Jacobson and Rosie are there, too. Come on." Alma hurried ahead, and the thought of food made Hetty catch her breath and follow.

After the meal, Alma, Hetty, Mrs. V, and Mrs. Jacobson stayed at the lunch spot to guard the supplies and rest. Everyone else had grabbed a bite of food and hurried back to Finnegans Point for the last loads.

Sun melted the snow off huge boulders. The rocks made a good place to sit and daydream. Glaciers, huge slabs of ice and snow, hung on the mountain not far from the trail. Hetty wondered if they ever turned loose and crashed down. Rosie had fallen asleep, so Hetty and Alma amused themselves by watching the never-ending line of people walking by. Hetty got her journal from the top of her pack and wrote about some of the Klondikers they had met along the trail.

"Read me what you've written, Hetty," Alma begged when Hetty started to put the book away. "I don't see people the way you do."

"When you write down details, you start to see more and more." Hetty opened the journal, turned back a page, and began to read.

Yesterday, two people walked ahead of us for so long, we struck up a conversation. The woman's pack held some strange shapes. She told us she and her husband were carrying a piano.

Alma laughed. "Wasn't that funny, Hetty? I couldn't believe it."

Hetty giggled and continued to read.

I asked her how that was possible. She said they had taken the piano apart and were carrying the pieces to Dawson. When they get there, they'll put the piano back together and sell it to one of the hotels or saloons. She said the piano pieces are wrapped in wool yarn, which she is going to knit into sweaters and sell. Not all of the Klondikers are looking for gold lying on the ground.

Hetty closed her journal and sighed.

"It's hard to believe there's gold lying on the ground, Hetty. And with so many people going to look for it, will there be any left by the time we get there?"

Hetty found that she cared less and less about gold and more and more about having a thief in their party.

When Rosie woke up, Mrs. V asked, "Hetty, Alma, do you two girls feel safe guarding supplies while Sophie and I take our first load on to tonight's campsite? I feel guilty staying here any longer."

"Of course we do," Hetty answered. "And I never get tired of resting." She watched as Mrs. V and Mrs. Jacobson, carrying Rosie and a backpack, disappeared around a bend.

"You keep an eye on our supplies, Alma. I watched where Eddie left his small pack. I'm sure it's where he keeps his personal things. I'm going to look in it for my locket."

"Are you sure that's a good idea?" Alma asked.

"I'll be careful." Hetty loosened the drawstring of the backpack Eddie had left with them and widened the top. Dirty clothes spilled out. Carefully she lifted out a pouch similar to the one where she kept her journal, her pencils, and her two books. "In for a penny, in for a pound," she whispered, and carefully opened the flap. She pulled out candles, matches, a jackknife, and some string. Nothing suspicious at all. She stuffed everything back inside.

Next, since she had time, she looked for the pack that Carl had been carrying. Opening it, she raised her eyebrows in surprise. Carl's clothes were on top, but unlike Eddie's, they were carefully folded, stacked neatly. She lifted them out, finding nothing else until she got almost to the bottom. There was a tin tobacco box. Did she dare open it? She looked up, thought she heard the soft thud of boots on the trail and people talking. Quickly but carefully, she put everything back in what she hoped was the same order and closed the pack.

"Find anything?" Alma whispered just as Papa and Mr. Jacobson appeared with a huge load.

"Only that Carl likes things neat and Eddie doesn't care," Hetty whispered, not mentioning the tin box. She wished she could have opened it and looked inside.

While Papa and Mr. Jacobson rested, Hetty and Alma got back on the trail. They caught up with Mrs. V and Mrs. Jacobson and walked until mid-afternoon, when they reached an obstacle that seemed impossible to cross. A waterfall had turned to ice as it spread across the trail, continuing down a steep bank so that on the right was a drop-off, on the left a cliff and the ice flow.

"Oh, my," said Mrs. Vasquez. "How can we possibly get over that?"

Sophie Jacobson shifted Rosie to her other hip. She looked tired. Carrying a baby as well as a pack had to be hard. Rosie seemed extra quiet, her thumb in her mouth, her big blue eyes staring at the trail, as if she, too, was wondering what they were going to do next.

Papa and Uncle Donall walked up, heaved a big sigh, and dropped the loads they were carrying. "Good thing I'm not a quitter," said Papa.

Mr. Jacobson stood beside them and whistled. "Whew, that's a challenge."

Soon all their party stared at the icy obstacle.

"Okay," Papa said, "I suggest we carry everything to this spot, then think about how to get over that ice flow." Papa found a small clearing off the trail and piled up what they had already carried. Everyone but Mrs. Jacobson and Rosie turned around and hurried back down the trail.

After all their loads had been carried to the icy crossing, the men studied the situation, watching how other Klondikers got past the hazard. Some climbed way up and around the waterfall of ice that spread across the trail. Others roped their goods and each other across.

Papa, Uncle Donall, and Mr. Jacobson cut small trees and built a wooden ladder to lay over the ice like a bridge. Hetty held her breath as Uncle Donall scrambled to the other side. If the ladder slipped, he'd fall down the embankment. He secured his end of the ladder to a tree, then asked all the women to cross, staying to help them off the ladder. Without a pack, Hetty scrambled across the ladder on all fours, holding tight, not looking down. Eddie laughed at her, but she didn't care. When she looked back, Carl, watching her, actually smiled. That was the first time Hetty had seen a real smile on his face.

Hetty watched as the other women followed. Sarah Lancaster climbed across as if she had done such tricks every day in San Francisco. Finally, the men carried load after load of their goods across. When they were done, they left the ladder there for other travelers to use.

By the time they got all their supplies to Pleasant Camp, it was almost dark. Hetty was exhausted and starving, and she didn't see how anyone could have the energy to cook. She was in the woods, searching for firewood, when someone grabbed her arm.

She looked up to see Carl glaring at her, his dark eyes flashing anger. "You messed with our things, didn't you? You looked in my pack."

Hetty's heart raced. What could she say? It was as if Carl had seen her snooping. "I—I—"

"Don't ever touch my stuff again, you hear me?" He cracked a branch over a rock, gathered the pieces of wood, and stomped away.

Hetty knew what she had done was wrong. But Carl acted as if he had something to hide. She gathered an armload of wood and hurried back to camp to find Andy Nickerson walking up to their fire.

The big man smiled his crooked smile and winked at Mrs. Vasquez. "There you are," he said. "I hoped you'd get across that ice all right. I just happen to have cooked extra—if you like beans."

Everyone groaned. They'd barely started their trip and already they were tired of beans and bacon, bacon and beans.

"Well, I did buy a salmon from a better fisherman than me." Mr. Nickerson held up a huge fish he had hidden behind his back, and everyone cheered.

"Oh, Moosejaw," Sarah said, "I'll love you forever."

"I made extra rice last night, thinking we'd be tired tonight." Mrs. Jacobson had set up her stove beside Mrs. V's. She smiled and handed a fussy Rosie to Carl. Carl's angry frown turned to a smile when he looked at his sister.

"This is Mama's birthday," Eddie announced. "Let's have a party."

"Alma, Hetty," Mrs. Vasquez said, "if you'll make some tortillas, maybe I can bake a cake. I'll stew some of the dried peaches to spoon over it."

"Will you marry me, Maria Vasquez?" Andy Nickerson said, his eyes twinkling. "I've not found moose to be very good company."

Everyone laughed, lost their fatigue, and pitched in to celebrate Sophie Jacobson's birthday. After dinner, Eddie and Carl gave their mother presents. Hetty was all eyes when Mrs. Jacobson opened Eddie's present.

"Oh, how pretty," she said, lifting pink glass beads and earrings from a box.

Eddie whispered to Hetty, "I found them in a trunk along the trail. Papa said they'd been thrown away. He was sure it was all right to take them."

Hetty knew exactly where he'd found them. She felt as if she should apologize to Eddie for thinking he had taken her locket. Carl's present was a small, perfect crystal he said he'd found in the river. He had fashioned a string into a holder for a necklace.

"I'm sorry the cake is so flat," Mrs. Vasquez apologized

as she cut it and handed out slices. "But an oven under a sheet of iron doesn't work so good."

"Only you could bake a cake on a campfire, Maria," Mrs. Jacobson said. "Thank you." Rosie sat in her mother's lap and clapped her hands as she stuffed cake into her mouth.

Hetty and Alma had started eating when Hetty noticed that Carl had disappeared. "I'll get Carl," she offered. "He's missing the cake."

"He's probably in the tent," Eddie said, reaching for his slice.

Hetty ran to the Jacobsons' big tent, thinking she should probably apologize to Carl. She lifted the flap and stepped in. "Carl, we're serving cake."

"Get out of here!" Quickly Carl put something behind his back. "You can't come in my tent without permission."

"I just did. What are you hiding?"

"Nothing. And if I was hiding something, it's none of your business."

Hetty stared at the tall, skinny boy. His dark eyes held anger—and what looked for all the world like fear. He stood up and came toward her. She stepped back, then scrambled out of the tent. Stumbling, she turned and ran back to the birthday campfire, not caring if Carl got any cake or not.

Suddenly she was sure she had suspected the wrong brother.

CHAPTER 6
A BATH AND OTHER ENTERTAINMENT

Klondikers had named this stopping place Pleasant Camp, because it was so good to rest after coming over the narrow trail studded with boulders, driftwood, and ice.

At breakfast the next morning, Mrs. Vasquez suggested, "I think the rain has let up. Let's stay here a day or two, do laundry and take baths. It's getting harder and harder to find firewood. Soon we'll have only enough to heat water for cooking—if that."

"Good idea," Sarah Lancaster agreed. "I'd love a bath."

"Me, too. I'm starting to stink." Hetty laughed.

"Don't let Eddie Jacobson hear you say that," Alma warned. "He'll never let you forget it."

"Alma, you go tell Sophie Jacobson our plan," Mrs. V said. "I'm sure she'll agree, since she was wishing we could rest. Then come back and help me with the laundry."

"Is it all right if I go with Papa to look for firewood?"

Hetty was used to talking to Papa often, and she had missed doing that.

Mrs. V agreed and Hetty, Papa, and Uncle Donall set out, Papa carrying his axe. Uncle Donall hurried ahead.

"Papa, I haven't seen you look at your watch today," Hetty said. "Did you put it in your pack?" Hetty knew Papa had a habit of looking at his watch often, even when the time didn't matter.

Papa sighed. "I've lost my watch, Hetty. I've looked everywhere. I guess I dropped it someplace."

Papa's face got red. He never had been good at lying. Uncle Donall was the brother who could tell any sort of tall tale and make you think it was the honest truth.

Hetty stared at Papa for a minute. "You think Uncle Donall took it, don't you?" she whispered. "Took it and lost it in a card game."

"No, Hetty, I don't think so. It wasn't worth much to anyone but me—or Donall. You see, my mother gave it to me after my father died. Inside, the case was engraved with my great-grandfather's name. Donall wouldn't part with it. He knows it's a family treasure."

Hetty kept quiet, waiting for Papa to speak again.

"I don't want to think Donall took it."

"Papa, someone took my locket, the one with Mama's photo in it. And Mrs. V's brooch is gone, not to mention her money. We have a thief with us, and it's either someone in our family or someone we've made friends with."

"No, no, Hetty, not our good new friends."

"I've wondered about Eddie Jacobson, or Carl—" Hetty remembered how guilty Carl had acted when she surprised him, how he had hidden something behind his back. Could Carl have stolen Papa's watch last night?

"Surely not. The Jacobsons are wonderful people."

"So is Uncle Donall. But—"

"We'd better get some wood, Hetty. I don't want to talk about this again. I'm sure I dropped my watch when I was crawling on the ladder across the ice or—or—sometime."

When Hetty and Papa returned to camp with an armload of chopped tree trunks and limbs, Mrs. Vasquez had a fire crackling and water heating for laundry.

"Donall brought wood, and then Mr. Nickerson brought me a load of wood while you were gone. Wasn't that sweet of Andy?" Mrs. V's face was so brown, it was hard to tell when she was blushing, but Hetty would have sworn she was now.

Andy Nickerson was courting Mrs. Vasquez!

"I told Sarah to go ahead and bathe," Mrs. Vasquez said. "Come and help Alma and me with laundry, Hetty."

"I have a headache," Hetty pleaded. "Do you mind if I help later?"

Mrs. V nodded, and Hetty ducked into the tent. She had hoped for a few minutes to herself, but she could hear splashing behind the blankets hung in one corner of the tent.

"Yoo-hoo," Sarah Lancaster called out from the makeshift bathing room. "Who is that?"

"It's Hetty. Does the bath feel wonderful?"

"We only get three inches of warm water, but I think it's the best bath I ever had." Sarah started to sing: "'Tell me, do you love me? For that's the sweetest story ever told.'"

Sarah didn't have a very good voice, but she didn't seem to care. Hetty smiled, knowing Sarah had been charmed by Uncle Donall. Did she love him? Hetty thought it would be risky to fall in love with her uncle. He was so unreliable about everything. And he hated being tied down by a job or even by an invitation to dinner. Hetty hoped that Sarah wouldn't get her heart broken.

Hetty spread out her bedroll, took a canvas pouch from her pack, and lifted out her journal and a pencil. What she really planned to do for a few minutes was write. She closed her eyes to think about Papa's watch being gone.

I read a story once about an ostrich, a bird who sticks its head in the sand, thinking it is safe from any danger it can't see. Papa is often like that ostrich. He refuses to believe something, hoping that will keep it from being true. If Uncle Donall took Mrs. V's money and used it to gamble at cards, as I fear he did, he must be losing a great deal. My heart breaks to think this, but I have to face the truth.

Yet even I cannot believe that Uncle Donall would have taken my locket, Mrs. V's brooch, or Papa's watch—inexpensive things that mean so much to us. To be fair to Uncle Donall, I will list others who might be our thief. (How strange that I have called him "our thief." I must ask others around us if they have lost anything.)

One of the Jacobsons: *Each time something has disappeared, the Jacobsons have been camped near us. One of them could have found an opportunity to slip into our tents and take things, but I am most suspicious of Carl. He is never friendly, and last night he was surely hiding something from me.*

Andy Nickerson: *He is often in our camp. Is he really courting Mrs. V, or is he only pretending to do so to cover his tracks as he takes things little by little?*

Sarah Lancaster: *I must list her. But if she is rich enough to live on Nob Hill, she could buy a dozen lockets or brooches or watches much finer than ours. Is it possible she is not rich? What if she made up the story of living on Nob Hill? Might she have the idea that Uncle Donall is a rich gambler, a good "catch" for a husband?*

Hetty could hear the soft sounds of Sarah getting dressed. She smiled at the idea of Sarah thinking Uncle Donall was rich.

Hetty looked up as Alma stepped into the tent. "Are you feeling better, Hetty? Mama gave me a break from washing clothes. This is a good chance to do some exploring."

"I'm too tired," Hetty begged off. "And you can see I'm writing."

"You don't have to get snippy."

"I—I'm sorry, Alma." Hetty glanced at the blankets behind which Sarah was humming. She lowered her voice to a whisper. "Someone took Papa's watch."

Alma sat down by Hetty so they could speak softly. "I'm not surprised to hear that. This morning when I searched my pack for a clean dress, I realized Miss Pittypat was gone. I can't find her anywhere."

"Oh, Alma, someone took Miss Pittypat?" Miss Pittypat was a doll with a real china head that Alma's father had given her for Christmas when she was four. The doll was precious to her. "Who on earth would steal a doll?"

"I don't know, but I miss her already. Hetty, I hate to suspect Donall as much as you do, but when Mama and I had the store, lots of young men came in. They bought all sorts of silly things for their girlfriends. Even dolls."

Hetty kept on thinking, but she put aside her journal. While Mrs. V bathed, she and Alma hung wet clothes on rope that Papa had strung around camp. After lunch, it was finally their turn for a bath. They bathed, washed each other's hair, and then scrubbed their dirty clothes in the bathwater. Hetty felt like a new person, sparkling clean and wearing a fresh dress. She and Alma stepped outside to help finish the good dinner Mrs. Vasquez had said she was starting.

"Look, girls. Andy brought me a starter of sourdough. Tomorrow I'm going to make sourdough pancakes for breakfast." Mrs. V held out a fruit jar of bubbly-looking dough.

"The dough is fermented," Andy Nickerson said. He'd made himself comfortable on a folded blanket by the campfire. "You mix a portion with flour and water to make pancakes or biscuits. They'll rise without yeast or baking soda. Up in the Yukon, we use the dough so much, folks call us old prospectors Sourdoughs."

"So you're a Sourdough?" Hetty asked.

"Sure am. I've been up here looking for gold for three years."

Hetty didn't want to hear that. "Haven't you found any? We heard you could pick up gold nuggets right off the ground."

"Not much, only gold dust. 'Course, I'm pretty unlucky. At least, I have been up till now." Andy Nickerson looked at Mrs. V and smiled. He was definitely courting, Hetty thought.

"I'd say anyone who'd been kicked by a moose is unlucky," Alma added. They had gotten used to Mr. Nickerson's face.

"Or dumb." Andy Nickerson tossed his head back with

a big, deep roar of a laugh. Once you heard it, you felt like laughing yourself. Even Hetty, with all she had on her mind, smiled.

❧

The second day they spent at Pleasant Camp was the most leisurely of the trip so far, Hetty decided. Despite her worry about a thief among them, she and Alma wandered around watching the hundreds of people. The sun came out in full force, which helped cheer them up.

Belinda Mulrooney rode by them on a fine black horse, followed by several men and a string of pack mules.

"Miss Mulrooney, hi," Hetty called. "What happened? Did you find the man who cheated you?"

Miss Mulrooney waved and turned her horse toward Hetty and Alma. "I most certainly did find him—back in Dyea, getting ready to cheat other travelers." She smiled. "This is his horse."

"*His* horse? Did you steal his horse?"

"No, I took it and told him he'd get his horse back when his men have gotten my supplies over Chilkoot Pass and on their way to Dawson."

The spirited horse danced in circles. Belinda Mulrooney laughed, and Hetty and Alma clapped their hands. "Good for you, Miss Mulrooney."

"By the way, Miss Mulrooney, did you notice anything

missing from your belongings when you returned to Finnegans Point?" Hetty asked.

"No, I don't think so. Why do you ask?"

"Just wondering," Hetty said. "Good luck."

"She has so many crates," Alma said, watching Miss Mulrooney ride away, "she might not notice if something is missing."

That night, there was a small Wild West show put on by the couple Uncle Donall had met in Dyea. The man, Arizona Charley Meadows, and his wife, Mae, had been star performers in Buffalo Bill's Wild West Show. Mrs. V had urged Hetty and Alma to go see the show while she and Moosejaw cleaned up supper dishes. Holding hands, Hetty and Alma skipped and ran toward the noise of town to find the crowd that was gathered around the two entertainers.

"Look at Mr. Meadows' long curly mustache," Alma whispered. "And his wife is so pretty."

Arizona Charley wore leather pants and a leather vest. All along the outside of the pant legs and the vest ran leather fringe. When Charley moved, the fringe moved.

For their first trick, Arizona Charley stood some distance from his wife, who was wearing a pink dress with masses of ruffles and petticoats. Mae held up playing cards one at a time. Charley took careful aim, then shot the pips off each card. The crowd oohed and aahed with every shot.

"What if he misses?" Hetty whispered to Alma and to Eddie, who had found them.

"Then he'll be looking for another wife," Eddie said. "Want to volunteer?"

"Not me," both girls agreed.

"Where's Carl?" Hetty asked Eddie. She knew she couldn't always keep track of Eddie's brother, but she wondered why he never seemed interested in having fun.

Eddie shrugged. "He started out with me. I guess I lost him."

They watched until the show was over. As the crowd drifted away Hetty spotted Uncle Donall talking with Arizona Charley and Mae. They ducked inside the Meadowses' big tent.

Hetty didn't have to guess what they were going to do next. They'd get out a new pack of cards, one without holes, and start a game. Hetty couldn't help but think that Arizona Charley might be as skilled at playing poker as he was at shooting.

Even though it was early evening, Hetty and Alma hurried back to their camp. Weaving between tents, they caught sight of Moosejaw.

"Good night, Mr. Nickerson," Hetty and Alma called.

"Girls, stop for a minute. I need to ask you a question." Mr. Nickerson stepped closer, holding up his candle. It cast flickering shadows over his misshapen face.

"This evening, Alma's mama sent me to my tent for my

big knife so we could skin out some squirrels I bought from an Indian man."

Hetty had seen Andy Nickerson's knife. She knew the one he meant. She had a sinking feeling all over that didn't come from being tired.

"Seems my knife is missing," Mr. Nickerson continued. "I don't suppose you've seen it anywhere."

"No. No, we haven't, Mr. Nickerson," Hetty answered.

"Well, if you see it, let me know. I'd hate to lose that knife. Good night, girls." In a moment he had disappeared into the shadows.

Hetty grabbed Alma's hand and squeezed. She had a new idea, and it frightened her. Maybe there were two thieves coming to their tents—one who took trinkets, one who took knives and money. But if someone was sneaking around with a big hunting knife, Hetty knew she had better be more careful about asking questions.

CHAPTER 7
SHEEP CAMP

When Hetty and Alma got back to the campsite, they found Jack London sitting at the fire with Mrs. V and Papa. Hetty put aside her fear about a thief with a knife.

"Jack," she cried, "I thought you'd be in Dawson by now."

"He was," Mrs. Vasquez teased. "But he walked all the way back here to get some of my good cooking."

"That's right." Jack went along with the joke. "I don't know anyone else who can bake desserts on a sheet-iron stove." Jack held a dried-peach pastry from the evening's dinner and was stuffing it into his mouth. When he'd eaten the last crumb, he said, "Have you been writing, Hetty?"

Hetty knew Jack was going to ask her that. She wished she had the nerve to read him some pages from her journal, but what she'd written was too personal and mostly about the thief in their midst.

"A little. But I'm awfully tired at night."

"If we get a snowstorm, you can catch up. I admit I'm not writing my thousand words a day, either. Some nights I'm too tired. But I'm always writing in my head, aren't you?"

Before Hetty could say yes, she was surprised to see Sarah Lancaster show up out of the darkness. Why wasn't she in town with Uncle Donall?

"Oh, Jack, would you sign your autograph in my own journal?" Sarah slipped into the tent and returned with a flower-covered book. "I'm just so sure you'll be a famous author someday. I can say I knew you. And I'll already have your autograph."

"Famous?" Jack laughed at the idea. He shook his head, but he signed his name in a sprawl across a blank page. "Rich, maybe—though I can already see that searching for gold is going to be hard work. I might settle for being rich with stories." Jack looked at Hetty and smiled. His sea-blue eyes, dark in the evening light, sparkled.

Jack stood up. "Thanks so much, Mrs. Vasquez. I heard that a poet was reading some of his verse tonight at the saloon. You want to go with me, Mr. McKinley?" Jack hooked his arm through Papa's and pulled him away from the campfire. Hetty knew it didn't take much persuasion to get Papa to go hear someone else read.

"Sarah?" Papa invited. "Go with us?"

"No, thanks, Glen. I'm a bit tired." Sarah slipped into

the tent, making Hetty wonder if she and Uncle Donall had had a falling out.

"Good luck, you *cheechakos.*" Jack waved as he and Papa left.

Hetty laughed at Jack calling them *cheechakos,* the name the native Indian people had given to those making the trip to the Yukon for the first time. *Cheechakos,* Sourdoughs, Yukoners, Klondikers. Nicknames caught on fast here. Hetty got her journal from the tent and sat beside the campfire to write down all the names. Then she wished *she'd* gotten Jack's autograph.

The next morning, Hetty and Alma helped Mrs. Vasquez finish packing while Papa, Uncle Donall, and Sarah Lancaster started on the trail to Sheep Camp with their first loads. Sarah had bought two sleds in town—one for her and one for Uncle Donall. She said that a sled should be easy to pull and they could move larger loads again. Hetty wished she had a camera to take a photograph of Sarah Lancaster pulling her sled by two leather straps strung over her shoulders. Sarah still wore her big picture hat, although the violets looked a bit forlorn and the tulle roses weren't as puffy.

The air got colder the higher Hetty and Alma climbed onto the mountain, and the trail became steeper. Hetty pretended to stop and look up at the cliffs for mountain sheep. Really she had to stop to catch her breath. The trail still followed the bed of the Dyea River. Here the river widened out again, so the fast-moving water was shallow and they could cross on stepping stones. Earlier, they had had to cross the river on slick logs tied together. Hetty always struggled to keep her balance with a pack on her back. She surely didn't want to fall and get wet. Then she'd really be cold.

All the trees alongside the trail had been cut down for firewood. The trees they could see in the distance didn't grow as high as the ones in the lower elevations. The sky was solid gray-white. Clouds drifted low and foggy. Snow fell off and on all day as they moved load after load closer to Sheep Camp, their destination for the night.

In the early afternoon, Hetty was surprised when she and Alma caught sight of Papa, resting beside the trail. "Are you all right, Papa?" she asked, worried.

"Fine, Hetty, fine." But Papa coughed and coughed before he got up and followed the trail again.

"I'm afraid Papa is getting sick," Hetty said to Alma. "I think we'd better take another rest day at Sheep Camp so he can get better."

"Everyone says we'd better get over the pass before the weather gets any worse." Alma bent and shifted her load to ride higher on her shoulders.

The trail got narrower and narrower. Hetty stopped

worrying about Papa and concentrated on putting one foot before the other. Her pack seemed to grow heavier with every step. She bent over more and more.

A while later she looked up to see Uncle Donall and Sarah, pulling empty sleds, heading back down the trail for what they thought would be the last load before they made the push to Sheep Camp.

"Did you see Papa?" Hetty asked.

"We told him to guard the supplies and rest," Uncle Donall said. "He seems awfully weak. We've agreed to stay at Sheep Camp until he's stronger."

When something worried Uncle Donall, it was past time for Hetty to worry. She forgot her aching shoulders and walked faster until she found Papa leaning on a stack of flour bags next to the huge piles of supplies everyone had carried that far.

"Your mother's taking the first load to camp, Alma," Papa said. "She didn't mean to leave you behind, but she wanted to get dinner started."

When Hetty and Alma finally crossed the swift-running river to Sheep Camp, bringing in their first loads, they were amazed at how many people were there. Hetty had thought the other camps were crowded, but here she would bet there were forty or fifty permanent tents in addition to those of the Klondikers moving through—a real town by Alaskan standards. Hetty wished she and Alma could look around, but they quickly unloaded their packs near the campfire Mrs. V had started, then went back down the trail for a second load. There were still hours of hauling to do.

It was after dark when Uncle Donall and Sarah brought in the last loads. Papa, without a pack, walked slowly beside them. He sat by the fire while Uncle Donall and Sarah helped Hetty and Alma set up the tents and put supplies inside. Uncle Donall insisted Papa go to his tent and lie down. Then Uncle Donall and Sarah hurried off, hand in hand, to look around.

Hetty couldn't remember Uncle Donall ever bringing a woman home with him for dinner, either when Mama was cooking or when Hetty took over meals. Sarah wasn't the burden Hetty had thought she'd be when she first joined their party. She was doing her share of the work, and she was always laughing or smiling. Maybe Hetty should worry about Sarah, warn Sarah that Uncle Donall was unreliable. She didn't think, though, that without proof she could tell Sarah the rest of her suspicions—that he might also have stolen Mrs. Vasquez's money.

Hetty hated thinking her uncle was a thief, but the idea came easily. Yet surely the other things that had gone missing since the beginning of the trip couldn't be wagered in cards, could they? Habit made Hetty reach for the locket around her neck. Maybe Uncle Donall could bet a good knife in a card game instead of money, but the idea of grown men playing cards for Miss Pittypat made her smile, despite her worry.

"Why are you smiling, Hetty?" Alma asked as they got out tin plates and cups for the evening's meal.

"I'm not sure if I should worry about Uncle Donall or Sarah." Hetty described her image of grown men playing cards for a doll, and the two girls had to laugh. But Hetty laughed to hide her tears as she added Papa to her worry list. They could all hear him coughing from inside the tent.

"Take Glen this cup of strong tea, Hetty," Mrs. V said. "I don't like the sound of that cough. Tell him I put a splash of whiskey in the cup, for medicinal purposes, mind you."

Hetty carried the tea into Papa's tent. He lay on his bedroll. "How do you feel, Papa?" Hetty had never seen Papa look so pale and gaunt. She set the cup beside him.

"Don't worry, Hetty. My throat just feels a bit raw from such cold air. You run along and let me sleep before dinner."

When Hetty stepped back outside the tent, she saw Mr. Jacobson standing at their fire. "Is Glen all right?" he asked her. "He didn't look good when we passed him earlier. We're that second tent over if you need anything." Mr. Jacobson pointed to their camp.

"Papa needs extra rest," Hetty said. "We're going to stay here until he gets a little stronger."

"We've decided to stay a couple of days, too. Sophie is exhausted. And Rosie is awfully fussy." With a worried shake of his head, Mr. Jacobson turned and walked away.

The girls had gotten used to seeing Moosejaw sitting at their campfire. Tonight he was stirring flour into some of the fermented sourdough mixture to make biscuits. Smelling the food cooking, Hetty felt sick to her stomach as well as sick at heart. She was worried about Papa, about Uncle Donall stealing money, about him or another thief taking things . . . about the trip they had thought would be fun turning into the hardest work any of them had ever done.

"If Mr. Nickerson is going to help you cook, Mama," Alma begged, "can Hetty and I look around Sheep Camp for a few minutes?"

Mrs. V nodded, hardly looking up from frying bacon.

"Come on, Hetty," Alma whispered. "I know you're worried, but looking around will cheer you up."

Alma grabbed Hetty's hand and took off before Mrs. V thought of another chore for them to do. Their first stop was the Jacobsons' tent. Even though Hetty still had Eddie on her suspect list, he was so much fun that she liked spending time with him. Besides, he might let something slip, like "Rosie just loves her new doll."

"Psst, Eddie," Alma called at the front flap, "are you in there? Come into town with us."

A crash behind them made them swing around. There was Eddie, laughing at their expense as he stacked up the load of firewood he'd dropped from his arms. "What are you doing here?" he asked.

"We were looking for you," Hetty said. "We wanted to see if you could go into town."

Eddie looked around. "Sure, let's go. Carl can finish helping Mama." He took off running.

Hetty and Alma trotted after him. Hetty was tired, but she wanted to see everything and write it down in her journal. Maybe she'd write a story about this trip someday.

Sheep Camp's muddy streets were crowded with sweaty men who had walked all day carrying eighty-pound packs. Now they were laughing and shouting at each other. Dogs howled and barked, very few of them tied up. Horses wandered the streets, most so thin that their ribs showed through their skin. Their coats were dull and covered with mud.

"Who owns these horses?" Hetty asked a boy who was trying to run the horses away from a wooden building. The front of the building bore a huge cloth sign crudely lettered with the words *PALMER HOTEL*.

"No one owns 'em. Folks who started out with horses and pack mules leave 'em here. Horses can't climb much farther. People who wanted to ride horseback all the way, or have horses and mules carry their packs, took the other route—White Pass Trail. It's longer, but it's not as steep as Chilkoot." The boy stopped talking to shout at a horse, "Go on! Git, I told you!" When the horse trotted away, he turned back to Hetty. "My name's Tom Palmer. What's yers?"

"I'm Hetty. These are my friends, Alma and Eddie. We're from California. Do you live here?"

"Sure do. Come on, I'll show you around." Tom let them peek into the Palmer Hotel, which he seemed to think was some kind of paradise in the wilderness. The hotel was one big room, and Hetty couldn't imagine sleeping there with the forty people Tom said they had every night.

Tom led them on a quick tour of Sheep Camp. "There are more hotels here. None better'n ours, but all as crowded. Sheep Camp is the last good place to rest before climbing Chilkoot Pass."

Hetty listened to every story Tom told. He was like a walking newspaper, full of information. Eddie, Alma, and Hetty kept the questions flying until they knew all there was to know about the bustling town of Sheep Camp.

"Is—is there a jail here?" Hetty asked. "A sheriff?" She didn't know why she was asking, or what she thought she was going to do if Tom said yes.

"No, the Yukoners keep law and order among themselves. They usually whip criminals." Tom grinned at Hetty. "Why did you ask that? Are *you* a thief or a murderer?"

"Just wondering." Hetty felt Alma squeeze her hand. "We have to go back to our camp, Tom. Thanks for the tour." Hetty took off, knowing that Alma would follow. Eddie could stay with Tom if he liked.

The first thing Hetty did when they got back to camp was to go inside the tent and check on Papa. He was asleep.

In the guise of covering him up, Hetty ran her hand along his waist. He wore the money belt under his clothing, and it still felt fat with their grubstake. She was sure that the money they'd lent Uncle Donall was gone, and that, if Uncle Donall had taken Mrs. Vasquez's restaurant money, it was gone, too. Hetty just hoped they'd all have enough to live on in Dawson until they discovered gold.

"Hetty, where are you?" Alma called, sticking her head into the tent. "Mama needs us to serve supper and then clean up. She's going over to help Mrs. Jacobson. Rosie is awful sick."

Chapter 8
Another Thief

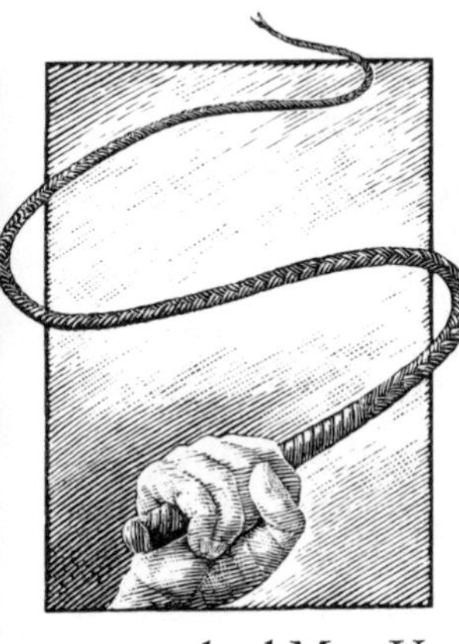

Rosie Jacobson had typhoid fever. Hetty and Alma wanted to go to the Jacobsons' tent with Mrs. Vasquez, but she said no, there was nothing they could do to help.

"What's wrong?" Sarah Lancaster asked. She and Uncle Donall surprised Hetty by coming back for supper. They watched Mrs. Vasquez hurry away.

"Little Rosie Jacobson has typhoid," Hetty explained, dishing up beans and rice for everyone.

"Lots of people are sick with one thing or another." Andy Nickerson placed one of his sourdough biscuits on each plate. "But this is the first case of typhoid I've heard about on the trail this autumn. I've seen many a feller die of it with no doctor available."

Hetty felt her stomach tighten. "You think Papa has typhoid?"

"No, I think he just has a bad cold. He should be

careful it doesn't turn into pneumonia, though," Andy Nickerson said.

Hetty thought about how sweet little Rosie was, how she loved to hold Rosie and tickle her and watch her giggle.

"If it's possible, Mama will make her well, Hetty," Alma said, just as Hetty was thinking the same thing. The two girls had been together so much, they seldom had to explain thoughts, knowing they were often the same.

"I'm so glad you came on this trip, Alma," Hetty said softly. "I can't imagine being here without you."

"Me, either," Alma agreed. "I was so afraid we'd have to turn back after Mama's restaurant money was stolen. Mama is worried about your father paying our way."

They ate in silence until finally Uncle Donall set down his dish for Hetty to wash and held out his hand to Sarah. "Coming, Sarah? There's a great game going together at the saloon."

"I don't think so, Donall." Sarah sounded tired, or sad. "I think I'll go to bed early tonight." She watched Uncle Donall leave without her.

"You aren't getting sick, are you, Sarah?" Hetty asked.

Sarah shook her head, but she got up, leaving her food half eaten, and walked toward the tent. As she raised her hand to lift the tent flap, a gleam caught Hetty's eye. She looked harder at Sarah's hand.

"What a beautiful ring, Sarah," Hetty said. "I haven't seen you wear it before."

"It's new, Hetty. Your Uncle Donall gave it to me. Isn't it pretty?" Not waiting for an answer, Sarah ducked into the tent.

"You think they're engaged?" Alma whispered as soon as Sarah was gone.

"I don't know. Where would Uncle Donall get such a ring, Alma? It looks expensive. I can't bear the thought that Uncle Donall is a thief, but the idea won't go away. If he gets caught, he'll be flogged or—or sent back home. Well, back to San Francisco."

Hetty didn't sleep much that night. She turned over and over. Usually she was so tired that she didn't notice the hard ground, but now a list of worries she could count like sheep kept her awake: Little Rosie being sick. Uncle Donall being a thief. He and Sarah being engaged. Hetty could hear Papa coughing in the next tent. Mr. Nickerson said that with no doctors up here, a lot of people died. She couldn't imagine Papa dying. What would she do without him?

The next morning, Eddie Jacobson slapped the side of their tent to wake them up. "Hetty, Alma, get dressed. Come on. Some Klondikers caught a thief. There's going to be a public flogging in a few minutes."

A thief? Was it Uncle Donall? It didn't take long for

Hetty and Alma to yank off their nightgowns and throw on their clothes over the underwear they always slept in.

"Who is it?" Hetty sat on a stump outside the tent to pull on her boots. Her fingers trembled so badly that she could scarcely tie the laces.

"I don't know. Tom just came and told me a man was caught."

"How is Rosie?" Alma asked, making Hetty ashamed not to have asked about that first.

Eddie bit his lip and his face lost its excitement. "Mama made us come and sleep in your papa's tent last night. It's so quiet in our camp, I'm afraid to ask."

Hetty peeked back into her tent. Mrs. Vasquez's bed was empty, as was Sarah Lancaster's.

The morning was terribly cold. Hetty wrapped her muffler around her stocking cap and over her face, leaving only her eyes showing. Suddenly all her worries overwhelmed her. She kept blinking tears from her eyes, wondering if tears could freeze. Twice she stumbled, and Eddie and Alma had to help her up.

"I—I'm just so cold." That wasn't her problem, but that was all she wanted to say.

A huge crowd had gathered near the saloon. Hetty, Alma, and Eddie pushed and wove their way into the middle of the crowd. Eddie jumped up and down to see what was happening. Finally, Hetty stood on tiptoe and got a glimpse of the scene in back of the saloon. A stout, bearded man stood near a wooden pole, holding a whip. Another man was tied to the pole. His shirt had been removed so that his back was bare. When Hetty saw him, she stifled a scream. "Oh, that poor man."

The man was turned away from her, but his hair was the exact dark color of Uncle Donall's. He was so far away, Hetty couldn't be sure it was him. People pressed in on her, trapping her. Why did everyone want to see this? Why had Eddie brought her and Alma to see it? Hetty wanted to run, but she could hardly move. She looked again and caught a glimpse of several red coats near the front of the crowd. Some Mounties were watching, but they didn't seem to be interfering.

Hetty watched the bearded man raise his whip and bring it down on the thief's back. Once, twice. Again and again. The crowd murmured or spoke in soft voices. Otherwise, all Hetty could hear was the crack and thud of the whip, and the man's groans.

Soon Hetty was sobbing. "I don't want to see this. Let's go back." She tried to turn around, but the crowd kept her from leaving.

Alma hugged her. "You can't be sure it's him, Hetty," she whispered.

"You know who it is?" Eddie asked.

"No, of course not." Hetty's anger helped her get control. "It's just so terrible."

"So is stealing," Eddie said. "Look, there's your Uncle

Donall right up front, watching. Him and Miss Lancaster."

When the flogging was over, the crowd broke up and onlookers began to drift away. Hetty was so thankful to find the thief wasn't Uncle Donall, she hurried to her uncle and hugged him. He held her tight, and Sarah laid her hand on Hetty's shoulder.

"I'm sorry you came to see that, Hetty," Uncle Donall said. "Go back to camp."

Just then a young woman near Sarah screamed, "My ring! Here's another thief!" The woman was pointing right at Sarah's finger.

Sarah's face turned as white as fresh-fallen snow. She clasped her hand over the ring. Stepping back, she would have fallen had not Uncle Donall put out his arms to hold her.

"This woman is wearing my ring," the young woman screamed to anyone who would listen. "It disappeared two nights ago."

The man with the whip moved close to Sarah. "Is this true?" he asked. "Where did you get that ring?"

"I—I—" Sarah stepped out of Uncle Donall's arms and stared at him. "It was given to me."

Uncle Donall looked straight at the man. "I won the ring fair and square in a poker game." Then he looked at Sarah, his face as red as hers was white. "I'm sorry, Sarah. I didn't want to tell you."

A young man stepped up beside them. He turned to

the angry young woman, looking as if he might cry. "Trudy, I'm so sorry. I—I lost it. Donall McKinley is telling the truth. I lost the ring in a card game. I'd planned to win it back for you."

"This is terrible!" Sarah Lancaster twisted the ring round and round until she could slide it off. She handed it to the woman, Trudy, then glared at Uncle Donall. "I can't believe this, Donall. You told me the ring belonged to your mother." Sarah stomped off, leaving Uncle Donall staring at her back.

Hetty caught his eye. He was as dismayed as Hetty had ever seen him. He had lost more than money or a ring. Hetty didn't offer any condolences to her uncle. If he had lost the woman he seemed to care about, especially with such a blatant lie, it was his own fault.

"Come on, Alma," Hetty said, turning back toward their camp. "I'm not hungry, but Papa needs to eat. I'm going to cook some oatmeal. You'd better eat breakfast with us, Eddie."

"Thanks, but I'm not very hungry." When they reached the campground, Eddie left them, walking slowly toward his tent.

Mrs. Vasquez had built a fire and was boiling water. At the same time, she dabbed at her eyes with a handkerchief. She looked up at Hetty and Alma, her eyes red.

"Mama, what's wrong?" Alma asked, but both girls knew.

"Little Rosie Jacobson died this morning. Wasn't

anything we could do for her. We'll be burying her this afternoon."

"Here?" The word flew out of Hetty's mouth.

"Yes. There's no way her family can take her back home, or take her on to Dawson either."

That afternoon Hetty and Alma found their best dresses, the ones they had last worn when they served meals at the tent restaurant. Mrs. Vasquez put on her black wool dress, and Sarah Lancaster dressed in her navy-blue corduroy suit. Papa got out of bed and put on his best suit. They all wore heavy coats, since the service was outside.

Hetty couldn't remember if the sun had been out earlier, but as they walked across the snowy ground to a site behind Sheep Camp for the service, gray clouds piled up and up and a few flakes of snow floated down. A small crowd gathered around a shallow grave dug from the frozen ground.

Mr. Jacobson, Eddie, and Carl carried a tiny coffin built from wood they had bargained for in town. Setting it down near the grave, they opened the lid one last time. Rosie was dressed in a yellow dress with ruffles and ribbons. Ringlets of red hair framed her face. She looked as if she were sleeping. Hetty found herself leaning against Sarah Lancaster. Sarah put her arm around Hetty and held her tight.

Uncle Donall was at the service, too, but he stood on the other side of the grave, beside Papa, and never looked at Hetty or Sarah.

The Jacobsons had found a minister who had been on the trail with them, the Reverend Christopher Mortimer, to preach a short service. His words blurred together and all Hetty could think was how short Rosie's life had been. But happy. She had been a happy baby, and everyone had loved her.

After the Reverend Mortimer's words, Mr. Jacobson picked up his accordion and played "Amazing Grace." At the sound of the favorite hymn, Mrs. Jacobson started to weep. Tears slid down Hetty's face, and she made no move to stop them.

Just before Carl and Eddie closed the coffin, Sarah took her hand from Hetty's shoulder, reached up, and tugged a clump of cloth violets from her hat. She stepped forward, leaned, and placed the violets in Rosie's folded hands. The gesture touched Hetty and she sobbed.

Mrs. Vasquez pulled both Alma and Hetty to her soft bosom and held them tight until Mr. Jacobson, Eddie, and Carl lowered the coffin into the shallow grave. Then Hetty and her family walked the short distance back to camp, leaving the Jacobsons alone.

Mrs. Vasquez built up the fire, no longer trying to save wood. She did what she did best—cook. No matter how sad they felt, they had to eat or they'd all get sick. Papa sat close to the fire, quiet but looking a little stronger.

Hetty needed to be alone. She slipped away, heading for the few trees left on the opposite side of town, away from the gravesite. The sun sank low, all warmth gone from its rays. Shadows gathered around huge boulders that had rolled off the mountain years in the past. She sat on the cold granite, thinking she had no crying left in her, so she was surprised when tears streamed down her face again.

"Hetty?" A hand gently touched her shoulder. She took some deep breaths, sniffed, then found her handkerchief and blew her nose. She turned enough to see shiny black boots. Then, through her blurry tears, she saw a red coat, a Mountie uniform. She looked up at Colin Brandauer.

"What are you doing up here, Hetty?" Colin asked.

"I needed to be alone. The Jacobsons' baby died this morning. I've just come from the funeral service." She paused, not knowing what else to say.

"I'm sorry," he answered. "Lots of people will die before they get to Dawson."

"That doesn't make it all right."

"I didn't mean it that way. I—" He paused and took a deep breath.

"I thought I saw you this morning." Hetty filled in the silence. "Have you been over the pass already?"

"I've been walking the trail back and forth, helping people where I could. The Mounties don't have any authority to enforce laws here, but I watched the thief being flogged this morning. I'm sure you heard about it. We do the same thing in Canada."

"I was there. I saw it. Flogging seems harsh punishment."

"It takes harsh measures to keep law and order up here, where there are thousands of people half mad with the idea of getting rich."

Colin knew about thieves. How could she get information from him without telling him there was a thief in her own camp?

"What do you think makes people steal, Colin?"

Colin sat on a rock across from Hetty. He thought for a moment. "The usual answer is greed or envy, wanting something someone else has. Maybe for some people, it's fun—they want to see if they can get away with taking things. Some might steal to tease or to spite someone, to get back at them. Or out of desperation, because they don't know how else to survive.

"It's not something you should worry about, Hetty. You're too young to worry about thieves, about criminals. I'm sorry you had to see what you did today. A man being flogged is a terrible sight." Colin stood up. "Come on, it's getting dark. I'll see that you get back to your camp safely."

Hetty nibbled at her supper, then begged off cleaning duties. Sarah said she'd help clean up. Hetty hurried into the tent, got out her journal, and sat on her bedroll, glad she was alone.

By the flickering light of a candle, she wrote about all the sad and terrible things that had happened today—seeing the thief being flogged, thinking it was Uncle Donall, Sarah returning the ring that Uncle Donall had won in a poker game, Rosie's funeral. The writing didn't help her understand everything, but she felt it ease some of the pain.

She wrote about her talk with Colin, and then she turned to the page where she had listed suspects. She added a line about each person, trying to reason out why each would steal: Eddie for fun, Carl for spite or meanness, Uncle Donall out of desperation to pay his gambling debts. Sarah Lancaster had plenty of money and no reason Hetty could think of to steal their knickknacks. Remembering Sarah's tender gesture at Rosie's funeral, Hetty crossed Sarah off her list of suspects.

Mrs. V and Alma came into the tent and spread out their bedrolls, so Hetty put her journal under her blankets, blew out her candle, and lay down.

The tent had been silent for a few moments when Hetty heard Mrs. Vasquez stir in her bed and draw in a sharp breath. There was the sound of paper crackling softly, and then the flare of a candle being lit.

"Hetty, Alma, are you asleep? Come here," Mrs. Vasquez whispered, raising her candle to light their way. "The most surprising thing has happened. My money has returned. This package was under the bundle of clothes I use for a pillow, and I thought—I thought— Come and see."

Hetty and Alma slipped over to Mrs. V's space. She was staring at a paper packet, its red ribbon now hanging loosely around it.

"Let us see!" Hetty and Alma said together.

Mrs. V opened the packet again and counted the paper bills inside. "Seven hundred and fifty dollars! I lost only five hundred."

Hetty hardly knew what to say. She was delighted that Mrs. V's money had been returned. But now Hetty was positive that Uncle Donall had taken the five hundred dollars. Returning even more money, wrapped like a present, was his style. In Alaska, he couldn't get candy or flowers to place on top like he had when he returned Hetty's grocery money. He'd had to settle for a ribbon.

"Girls, I have a tin of cookies I've saved for a special time." Mrs. Vasquez tucked the money back into the packet and placed it under her bedding. "I think this will do. Let's sneak out and make a cup of tea."

A party? A party to celebrate the return of something that had been stolen? Hetty was certain that Mrs. V knew who had taken her money, just as surely as Hetty did. But neither of them was going to mention his name.

So much had happened today, but Mrs. V's money coming back topped the list of good things. However,

Hetty couldn't put the idea of a second thief behind her. She nibbled her cookies and sipped her tea, not able to stop thinking.

The sky had cleared, and millions of stars, more than Hetty had ever seen, looked down on their flickering fire and their tea party. Papa's tent was quiet, so he was probably sleeping. Neither Uncle Donall nor Sarah had come back from town.

Hetty resolved to talk to Uncle Donall, to ask him about the mysterious return of Mrs. V's money. He might not want to admit he'd taken it, but she'd make him talk to her.

CHAPTER 9
THE GOLDEN STAIRS

Snow fell during the night, a foot of snow, and heavy clouds threatened more to come. Hetty knew they had to move on right away or risk being snowed in at Sheep Camp.

Papa felt stronger and his cough had eased, which cheered everyone up. And when he said he thought they should push on for The Scales, the last stopping place before they climbed to the pass, the whole party agreed and started eagerly to pack. The last camp was called "The Scales," Papa told them, because it was where packers weighed the goods they were carrying and determined what to charge their customers. "I'm going to walk over and tell the Jacobsons our plans," Papa said. "All of you finish packing. Donall, you organize carrying the loads."

Sarah Lancaster seemed to have forgiven Uncle Donall for giving her a ring he had won in a poker game. While packing up, the two got into a snowball fight.

"Hetty and Alma, come be on my side!" Sarah shouted, hiding behind a huge pile of supplies.

When a snowball hit Hetty squarely in the stomach, she knew she had to have revenge. She ducked behind the bags and crates and wadded up a ball of wet snow. Taking aim, she knocked Uncle Donall's hat off. Both of them were surprised by the direct hit. Laughing, Uncle Donall ran after her. When he caught her, he tossed her into a snowdrift and rolled her over and over. Hetty shrieked and giggled.

"Children, children," Mrs. Vasquez called. "Save that energy. You're going to need it. Come and eat a good, hot breakfast. Our noon meal will be cold. And who knows about supper."

Reluctantly, Hetty stopped playing. While they were all eating big bowls of oatmeal with raisins, Papa returned. "The Jacobsons say they're going to wait until tomorrow to leave. Sophie said she can't leave little Rosie yet."

Smiles disappeared and they all got back to work. Soon they had their supplies packed and were ready to carry the first loads. Mrs. Vasquez said that she and Andy Nickerson would guard, since she wanted to visit with Sophie Jacobson before she moved on.

Feeling like pack mules again, Hetty and Alma got on the trail. "I can't imagine leaving a baby sister here. Can you, Alma?"

With a heavy heart, Hetty walked all day, back and forth, carrying load after load. An icy wind chilled them all. The trail got steeper and steeper. Snow, ice, and mud, churned to a slick mixture by hundreds of tramping feet, made every step uncertain and difficult. Time after time the heavy sleds got stuck, and Uncle Donall and Sarah had to pull and tug to get them loose and continue on.

By late afternoon, almost too tired to walk, Hetty and Alma lifted their last loads and set foot on the trail again. A short distance from Sheep Camp, they spotted a woman, her pack spilled beside her, lying motionless in a snowdrift near the trail. "Look, Hetty. That woman's in trouble." Alma and Hetty stumbled through the drift and knelt beside the woman.

"Ma'am, wake up, you have to wake up! You can't lie down. You'll freeze." Hetty brushed snow from the woman's arm and tugged at her.

"Leave me alone," the woman mumbled. "If I can just rest a few minutes, I'll be all right."

Alma bent down and shook her. "No. No, you won't. Stopping, sleeping, is the worst thing you can do." She and Hetty tugged and pulled, forcing the woman to sit up.

"Help," Hetty called. "Someone come and help us."

A steady stream of people walked by. A few looked in their direction, but no one came to help. Many of the Klondikers looked as if they were ready to give up, too. They put one foot in front of the other like sleepwalkers. Hetty had heard some counting steps, "One-two-three-four-five. One-two-three-four-five."

"We have to get her up and walking or she'll die." Alma looked around, but they had gotten separated from all of their party.

Suddenly, Hetty heard a voice calling to them. "Hetty, Alma, what's the matter?" Hetty looked up to see Sarah Lancaster, who had paused on the trail beside her empty sled on her way back to Sheep Camp for a last load.

"Sarah, thank goodness. You have to help us. This woman is going to freeze." Hetty turned back to the woman beside her. "Look, look, ma'am, help is on the way. What's your name? Are you alone?"

"Je-Jewel," the woman said. She was shivering, and her teeth clicked together. "Jewel Higgins. My husband told me to wait for him at Dyea, but I—I got tired of waiting."

The three of them were able to get Jewel Higgins onto Sarah's sled. They placed her pack so she could lean on it.

"I'll take her back to Sheep Camp and find someone to take care of her," Sarah said. "You two go on ahead and catch up to Glen. I'm worried about your papa, Hetty."

Alma and Hetty helped Sarah get the sled sliding on the snowy trail, then started walking. In no time, they met Uncle Donall. "Find Sarah, Uncle Donall," Hetty said. "She may need help." They explained, and Uncle Donall hurried away.

Hetty realized that Sarah Lancaster was lots stronger than she looked. Through the entire trip, she had hauled heavy loads right alongside Papa and Uncle Donall.

And lately, Hetty was seeing changes in Sarah Lancaster that she liked. Maybe Sarah would make a good wife for Uncle Donall. Maybe it would be good for Uncle Donall to settle down and get married.

As they walked the trail, crowded with Klondikers, Hetty repeated Colin's long-ago words in a rhythm, hoping she wouldn't find Papa lying in the snow. *Only the strong will survive. Only the strong, only the strong.* "You must get strong again, Papa. You must," she murmured. She walked a little faster, anxious to locate him.

About a mile from Sheep Camp, a huge slab of ice hung on the side of the mountain not far from the trail. Hetty hurried past it. Just beyond it, at the next bend in the trail, Papa sat on a boulder, staring at the river. He looked pale and exhausted.

"Are you all right, Papa?" Hetty asked, studying his face.

"Fine, I'm fine, Hetty. Just need to get a second wind. But I don't think we're going to get to The Scales tonight."

Daylight had faded by the time Hetty, Alma, and Papa reached the two-mile point for the day, a place called Stone House. A huge square rock the size of a small cabin stood sentinel beside the rushing river. To the right was a jumble of boulders, the remains of a rock slide.

"This is it, girls," Papa said. "I can't walk any farther. When the others come, we'll talk it over, but we're going to have to make a primitive camp here for the night. We won't even put up tents."

When Mrs. V and Moosejaw, then Uncle Donall and Sarah arrived, they agreed reluctantly. Moosejaw said he had always found this spot on the trail spooky. They gathered their supplies in a semicircle and simply laid out blankets on the ground. The next morning, Mrs. V said she never slept a wink. Hetty had been so tired that she knew she must have slept a few hours, but she had often woken to hear Papa coughing.

Putting packs back on was a kind of torture. Hetty was stiff and sore and vowed she'd never carry so much as a spoon across a room once they reached Dawson.

The trail climbed higher and higher, and fog surrounded them as if they had walked into the clouds. Finally they reached The Scales with their first loads. Hetty thought it must be the ugliest spot on earth. There was no vegetation, no wood for a fire, and huddled together everywhere were miserable people.

While Uncle Donall and Sarah took the sleds back to Stone House, where Moosejaw was guarding, Mrs. V, Alma, and Hetty staked out a small piece of ground, more mud than snow. They made Papa rest while they put up one tent and started a fire. Then Mrs. V went back for another load of supplies, leaving Hetty and Alma to stay with Papa.

"Look, girls," Papa said, pointing to the trail. "I *thought* I heard bagpipes, but then I told myself that maybe I still had a fever and was hallucinating."

Papa pointed to a group of men marching up the trail

wearing, of all things, kilts. Underneath the plaid skirts, the men wore trousers and boots, and they were fat with sweaters and fur coats and mufflers. On their heads they wore the Scottish hats called tam-o'-shanters. Behind them walked Native packers, carrying their provisions. Leading the strange parade, one man played a set of bagpipes. The eerie music floated across the camp and quieted the murmur of voices.

Once they had marched past, the Scottish men laughing and waving as if they really were in a parade, the camp fell silent for a moment and the clouds lifted. In the stillness, broken only by the whistling of the wind, Hetty heard another sound, faint, even stranger than bagpipes on top of a mountain.

"What's that, Papa? What's that noise?"

"People in pain, Hetty. Carrying load after load up and over the pass."

Clouds drifted away from the mountain pass and weak sunshine tried to break through. The snow-covered peak seemed to reach all the way to heaven.

"You're looking at the Golden Stairs," Papa said. "Men have cut steps in the snow and ice all the way to the top of the mountain. Fifteen hundred stairs. That's what we have to climb next to get over Chilkoot Pass."

Hetty saw a line of people, looking for all the world like a thousand ants, moving slowly up the face of the mountain. The moaning sound came from them.

Suddenly Hetty was scared. "Oh, Papa. Can we—can we do that?" Hetty shaded her eyes and stared at the mountain again.

"Hetty!" Alma screamed. "Your papa!"

Hetty turned her eyes away from the Golden Stairs only to see that Papa had collapsed beside the fire.

CHAPTER 10
THE BLIZZARD

Hetty didn't see anyone nearby who could help them. But Papa wasn't a big man, and as she and Alma half carried, half dragged him into the tent, Hetty realized that Papa was awfully thin. They wrapped him in his bedroll, then went back outside to heat water for tea.

"Mama will know what to do, Hetty. She should be here soon."

Alma mixed flour and water for tortillas and hung a pot of bean soup over the fire to continue cooking. "I'm glad she sent tonight's dinner and the cooking pots on the sled with Donall's first load."

All of a sudden, Hetty felt weak with all her worries—the thefts, Uncle Donall, now Papa so ill. She took a deep breath. She couldn't do any more for Papa right now, but maybe she could do something about the other problems.

"Alma, if Uncle Donall is the next one here, will you give me a few minutes alone with him?"

"Of course, Hetty. Come help me with dinner."

Hetty dampened her hands and reached for a ball of dough to pat into a thin circle. She'd keep busy until the rest of their party arrived. She couldn't keep her mind from bouncing round and round as she worked, so she planned what she was going to say.

Sure enough, Uncle Donall was the first to return. He staggered into camp with a groan, pulling a sled loaded heavier than ever.

"Papa is too sick to go get another load, Uncle Donall. You'll have to carry his share. But I have hot water ready to make tea. Sit down by the fire, rest, and drink a cup before you leave again."

"I'll do that, Hetty, thank you. What an insane way to travel—pulling or carrying load after load up this mountain. I heard that someone was going to build a tram line, but it will come too late for us to use."

Alma got up and went into the tent. Wind gusted, flickering the meager fire. Hetty pulled her coat tighter and sat quietly, letting Uncle Donall get warm, forming her thoughts. Finally she spoke. "Uncle Donall, I have some things I need to say to you. I—this may make you angry, but I don't care. You're the one who took Mrs. Vasquez's money, aren't you?"

Donall McKinley stared into his mug of tea, as if

answers were there. Hetty couldn't hold back tears. Crying left her frustrated, but she often cried when she was angry.

"Hetty, you've got me dead to rights. I had a losing streak. What could I do? I couldn't borrow from Sarah, could I? And I returned the money. With interest."

"That doesn't make it right!" Hetty bit her lip and took a deep breath. "How can you be so irresponsible? What if you'd lost all of Mrs. Vasquez's money? You know how hard she worked to make it back after it was stolen in Dyea. But I guess since you've borrowed money from me and Papa in the past, I shouldn't be surprised that you'd *borrow* from Mrs. Vasquez."

Usually Uncle Donall would have kept talking until he charmed Hetty out of her anger. This time he sat quietly, head bent, and listened. His silence encouraged Hetty.

"I shouldn't have to tell you what's right or wrong, Uncle Donall. You're supposed to set an example for me."

"Fortunately you took after your mama, Hetty. I've meant to tell you for a long time how much I admire the way you took over when your mother died. Emily was a wonderful woman, so good for Glen. Neither he nor I know how to manage money, Hetty. You know that."

"That's no excuse."

"You're right." Uncle Donall took off his hat and ran his hands through his hair. He pressed the back of his hand to his lips.

"Did you take my locket, Uncle Donall? And Papa's watch? And Mrs. Vasquez's brooch? Alma's doll? And Mr. Nickerson's knife? Did you sell them or put them into your poker games when you ran out of money?"

Uncle Donall looked at Hetty for the first time. His blue eyes were sad and he shook his head. "Of course not, Hetty. I know how much that locket meant to you, that it carried a photo of your mother. How could you believe I'd do that, or take any of those things?"

"The same way I could believe you'd take Mrs. Vasquez's money. A thief is a thief." Hetty knew she was being harsh, but she might as well get this all out in the open.

"Glen gave that locket to Emily when they were married. I remember how she treasured it. I didn't take it, Hetty. Maybe you just lost it."

"You know I'd never lose it."

"I know, Hetty. I know." Uncle Donall got up, set down his mug, and kissed Hetty on the top of her head. "I've got more trips to make. I'd better get to it. I think a storm is coming."

"Uncle Donall, promise me that you'll apologize to Mrs. Vasquez for 'borrowing' her money."

"I will, Hetty. I promise I will." Saying that, Uncle Donall started back toward Stone House. He disappeared in seconds.

Alma stepped out of the tent. "Your papa is sleeping, Hetty. Did Donall leave? What did he say?"

"He said he 'borrowed' your mother's money, and that tonight he'll apologize to her. But he said he didn't take the other things, and I believe him. I know there's another thief, Alma."

All that afternoon, load after load came in until everyone agreed they had only one more. While Hetty and Alma waited for the last of the supplies, the wind picked up. The late-afternoon sky turned dark gray. Ghostly clouds pressed lower and lower, closing in on their campsite. Alma looked at Hetty, and Hetty read her thoughts. The storm was going to catch her mother, Mr. Nickerson, Uncle Donall, and Sarah on the trail.

People were so crowded together on this small, flat piece of snow-covered ground that it should have been noisy. Instead, it seemed as if people were holding their breath. Waiting.

Hetty's skin prickled. She and Alma sat huddled near the fire, with nothing to do but wait. Then huge flakes of snow started to fall, fast and furious.

"I'm sure your mother will be here soon." Hetty made them each another cup of tea. She didn't really want it, but it was something to do. She watched tea leaves swirl in the hot water. Wind started to swirl snow around them in the same manner.

They had heard wolves howling in the distance the last two nights. Now the wind sent up a similar wailing, keening moan.

"I'm scared, Hetty."

"So am I, but there's nothing we can do but wait and keep the fire going. Let's get inside the tent."

"No, I'm going to wait here." Alma pulled her shawl tighter over her head and shoulders.

"I'll check on Papa." Hetty crawled into the tent. Papa was asleep, but his breathing was shallow and his face flushed. She piled her own blankets on top of his, knowing that sweating helps a fever. He didn't move.

"Please, Papa. Please be all right. A snowstorm has started. We can't leave for the pass tomorrow anyway, so we'll stay here until you feel better." To use up time, Hetty got out her journal and wrote by candlelight. Pouring her heart out in words soothed her. Finally she heard Alma shout, "Mama!"

Hetty pinched the candlewick, dropped her journal, and stepped outside the tent. Four snowmen staggered into camp—Sarah and Uncle Donall pulling their sleds, and Mrs. Vasquez and Moosejaw behind them, each roped to a sled. They carried the last of their supplies and set them in a semicircle around the camp.

"Oh, my goodness, I didn't think we'd ever get here," Sarah said. She set down her backpack and started unloading her sled. "I was afraid we'd walk right past you in this storm."

Alma brushed snow off her mother and hugged her. Mrs. Vasquez had a big smile on her face. "Fortunately,

Donall made me tie a rope to his sled, and then he led the way."

"But Sarah broke trail for that last stretch." Uncle Donall hugged Sarah.

"The Jacobsons are right behind us," Sarah added. "They said Colin Brandauer urged them to pack up and push ahead. He knew a storm was coming. And he found some Indian women to help carry their supplies."

"How is Glen?" Mrs. V asked. "Girls, make a big pot of tea. That fire is never going to last in this storm." Mrs. V quickly brushed the snow off her clothes and stepped inside the tent.

They never even tried to put up a second tent in the storm, but all moved into one. Even Mr. Nickerson brought in his bedroll so that they could pile his tent full of their things.

There were times during the evening that Hetty thought the wind was going to lift up the canvas tent and roll it away with them inside. But bags, barrels, and crates had been lined up against the tent walls to help hold it down. Sarah and Uncle Donall had hammered extra pegs into the ropes before they came in for the night.

Sarah kept joking and teasing as if being in this storm was the most fun she'd ever had. After supper, she and Uncle Donall started a game of cards by candlelight.

Hetty had to admit that their laughter was a welcome diversion from the howling wind. Uncle Donall even pulled out his harmonica and played softly between hands. Sarah sang off-key again, but when she hit a sour note, she just laughed. Hetty sat beside Papa, holding his hand. As long as the noise didn't keep him awake, she was glad for the music.

The storm lasted two days. To while away the long hours, everyone slept, read in the dim light of day, or played cards and talked. They took turns watching over Papa. Hetty and Alma played cat's cradle with some string they had in their packs. And Hetty wrote page after page in her journal, describing the entire trip and all her feelings.

On the morning of the third day, complete silence woke Hetty. Not that she'd gotten used to the howling wind, but its absence seemed strange.

She stuck her head outside the tent to see an all-white world. "We're going to have to dig out of here," she called to anyone who was listening.

Uncle Donall, Sarah, and Mr. Nickerson had been smart enough to bring shovels into the tent, along with as many of their things as would fit. Everyone turned out to shovel snow. They hadn't dug far before they heard someone digging in their direction. A moment later, Eddie Jacobson popped out of a snowdrift with a big grin on his face. "Hey, Alma, Hetty. Some storm, huh? Were you scared?"

"No, we just waited it out," Hetty lied. She had been a little scared, wondering if the snow would ever stop falling.

"I brought a rope with me. I'll tie it to your tent pole so we can go back and forth from our tent to yours."

Alma and Hetty, using the shovels they had brought to dig for gold, helped Eddie widen the path, packing walls of snow on either side.

"I have to check on Papa," Hetty said, throwing down her shovel. She really meant to rest, although she did want to see Papa.

"Me, too." Alma followed her.

They hurried inside the tent to Papa's side. "Papa, you're awake."

"His fever has broken," Mrs. Vasquez said. "He should start to get better now."

"Oh, Papa, the snowdrifts are ten feet high."

"Now, Hetty," Papa said, his voice weak but his smile big. "You know how you like to exaggerate."

"No, she's telling the truth, Mr. McKinley," Alma said. "Donall says it probably snowed only three feet, but the wind piled the snow into huge drifts."

"Yeah, we made a path between our tents." Eddie had followed Hetty and Alma into the tent, and now he stuck up for Hetty. "Papa sends his regards. Mama says we should cook dinner together to save on wood."

"Oh, that's a wonderful idea. We can make it a party." Sarah Lancaster had come into the tent to change into dry clothing. She ducked behind the blanket separating off her bedroll.

"I'm not sure Sophie Jacobson will be in the mood for a party," Mrs. Vasquez said, reminding them all that Mrs. Jacobson was grieving.

"Alma and I will go ask her, Mrs. V," Hetty said. "We'll have a small party. A quiet party. She'll know we don't mean any disrespect."

Hetty wasn't sure Sarah knew how to have a quiet party, but she and Alma pulled their coats back on and ran outside to find Mrs. Jacobson.

"I'll tell Pa and Carl the plans." Eddie picked up his shovel and went to look for his father and Carl.

Alma and Hetty walked along the snowy passageway. The Jacobsons' tent was quiet. They heard the thud and scrape of a shovel nearby, but couldn't see anyone.

"Anyone here?" Hetty called and got no answer. She lifted her finger to her lips, then motioned to Alma that she was going inside. She peeked around the tent flap and pulled it aside.

The Jacobsons' tent was bigger than theirs, and they had divided off rooms with rope and blankets. Hetty stepped inside. She peeked around the first blanket and saw two bedrolls and clothes that belonged to Mr. and Mrs. Jacobson.

She tiptoed to the second "wall" and pulled it aside quietly.

Sitting beside one heap of blankets was a good-sized tin tobacco box. She stopped. Listened. Alma would give her a warning if anyone was coming.

Quickly she knelt on the canvas floor, reached for the box, and, after a couple of tugs, slipped off the lid. Inside, some bundles were wrapped in newspaper. She took out the first. Slowly she unwrapped it, the paper crackling in the silence.

In her hand she held not a locket or a doll, but a pure white skull, two rows of sharp teeth grinning at her.

"Hetty, quick," Alma whispered. "Someone's coming!"

CHAPTER II
DANGER!

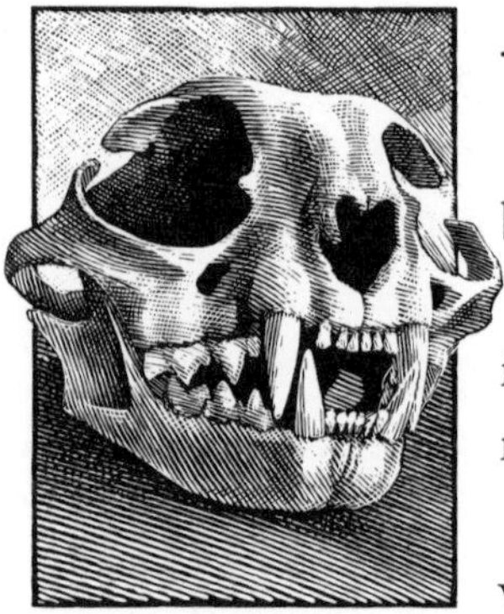

"What are you doing in our tent?" Carl blocked Hetty's escape, but she couldn't have run anyway. She was frozen in place, the skull still in her hand. "Don't break that." Carl reached for the skull.

"What is it?" Hetty knew she was in the wrong, but she'd stand her ground. Eddie stood behind Carl, looking amused at her getting caught. Behind Eddie, Alma raised her shoulders and indicated to Hetty that she couldn't stop the two boys from coming into their own tent.

"I'm glad there's *something* you don't know." Carl lifted the skull carefully from Hetty's hands, then knelt beside the tobacco tin.

"Aw, show her your collection, Carl," Eddie said. "What harm can it do? She's not going to break them."

Carl hesitated for a moment, then began to unwrap the contents of the box. "That's the skull of a cat." He indicated the one Hetty had been holding. "And this one is a mouse. A small dog. A snake. This is my best one. It's a porcupine." Carl set out each skull carefully.

Hetty felt her face heating up. "I—I'm sorry, Carl, for snooping into your private belongings. I, well, some things have disappeared from our tent. I—I thought—"

"That I took them? Why would I want any of your stuff? Don't we all have enough to carry?"

Hetty sat down and looked carefully at each clean, white skull. She owed Carl that. "Why are you carrying these, Carl? Seems strange when every pound counts."

"He studies them," Eddie answered for Carl. "He's going to be a doctor someday, specializing in skulls and brains. That's because his best friend died of a brain tumor before we left California."

"I'll get some more skulls in the Yukon. Maybe a wolf or a bear if I'm lucky." Carl packed his skulls back into the tin without saying anything else.

Hetty didn't know what else to say, either. If Carl planned to be a doctor, he must be a lot smarter than she was.

Hetty and Alma turned and slipped outside and through the tunnel of snow, with Eddie following them. "Eddie," Hetty asked, "why didn't you tell me about Carl's collection, what he was carrying across the mountain that was special to him?"

"I never thought about it. Carl doesn't like to talk

about his stuff. He stays to himself most of the time, so I leave him alone. Kids at school made fun of him because he's so smart."

"I think that what he wants to do is wonderful." Hetty looked around as they followed the passageway. "Where's your mother, Eddie? We still need to ask her if it's all right to have a little party to celebrate the end of the snowstorm."

"I'm sure it is, but I'll go find her, and I'll ask Pa, too." Eddie took off running.

"I don't know what to think, Alma," Hetty said when Eddie was gone. "I was so sure Carl was hiding our things. Now I can't believe he's our thief."

"Everything we find out leaves me more puzzled, Hetty."

"Let's watch everyone carefully tonight."

That evening Hetty decided, despite the cold, that she'd wear her next-to-best dress for the party. She found it in her pack, pressed her hands over the wrinkles, and put it on. Did she have time to write about Carl's skulls? She reached under her pillow, where she kept her journal. What—

There, polished like new, lay her locket atop her journal. She reached for it, then paused, hesitant to touch it for fear it would vanish again. If she had found it in her pack, mixed in with her dresses, she would have thought she'd only misplaced it—that all this time she had only imagined someone had stolen it. But, no, here it was, set out where she could easily find it.

Carefully she opened it. Her mother's smiling face stared back at her. Hetty's eyes filled with tears, and she let them flow.

"Hetty! What's wrong?" Alma came into the tent and hurried over to where Hetty stood.

Hetty held out her locket, the chain spilling through her fingers.

"Your locket! Where did you find it? What is going on, Hetty?"

Hetty fastened the locket chain around her neck and rubbed the shiny heart as it lay in the hollow of her throat. "I have a million questions, Alma, and not one answer."

The party that evening was small and quiet, but it was what they needed. All the Jacobsons came, even Carl, though he didn't talk to them. He ate his food and watched people but never said a word. Mr. Jacobson played some hymns and then some quiet—sad, Hetty thought—ballads on his accordion. They talked about Rosie, and what a joy she had been for her short life. They talked about home. The places they'd left behind. What they missed most. Mr. Nickerson talked about his life in Nebraska as a boy. He told them he hadn't lived in a real house for so long, he'd almost forgotten what it was like.

Hetty was sure it wasn't the kind of party Sarah and Uncle Donall had had in mind, but it seemed to suit everyone just to get together. Papa coughed some, but he looked a lot better. Hetty was so thankful. She had been afraid he had pneumonia.

The next morning dawned sunny and so bright that they had to put on the snow goggles they'd brought. Hetty wondered if she looked as funny as Alma did in the dark glasses that looked like huge fish eyes. But without them, Hetty had to squint her eyes so tight that she could scarcely see.

While everyone was outside, holding a cup of tea or coffee, Papa said, "I'm not sure we can carry all these goods to the top of that mountain. I'm feeling as limp as a wet glove." He nodded at the line of gloves hanging near the fire to dry.

"But, Papa, we have to," Hetty said. "Look how far we've come. We can't turn back now. You can't give up, Papa. This trip was your idea."

Hetty didn't think she *could* turn back. As hard as climbing the Golden Stairs was going to be, curiosity was taking charge of her. She knew what lay behind. She wanted to see what was ahead. "What happened to your sense of curiosity, Papa? Don't you want to know what's on the other side of Chilkoot Pass? Don't you want to write stories about the goldfields?"

"My curiosity is just fine, Hetty." Papa smiled at her. "It's my back and my legs that want to give up. Let's see how much money we have. Maybe we can hire packers to take us over the pass and on to Lake Lindeman. I can't pull my weight anymore, and I hate being a burden to everyone."

The idea of someone else carrying the packs sounded wonderful. The cost was scary. "Eddie said the Native people are charging fifty cents per pound." Hetty did some quick ciphering on the palm of her glove. "That's about a thousand dollars apiece for Uncle Donall and us, for Mrs. V and Alma, and for Sarah."

Papa nodded. "I know." He did look tired—as if he couldn't even carry a pencil and paper to write his newspaper articles.

"Maybe we can stay here until you're stronger," Hetty suggested.

"The weather is only going to get worse." Uncle Donall pushed up a pile of snow with the toe of his boot. Hetty knew he didn't have the patience to wait long.

Sarah Lancaster tossed the remainder of her tea into a snowdrift. "I have the solution to this problem. I'm carrying a lot of money. I'll help you hire the Native people."

"But, Sarah—" Mrs. Vasquez and Papa spoke together. "We can't—"

"You can. If I'm going to be a member of this family, I should invest in our future." Sarah Lancaster took off her picture hat and set it on a stack of flour bags. Her reddish-brown hair, an untidy nest on top of her head, spilled out ringlets around her face. Her green eyes were smiling as if she had a secret.

Uncle Donall stepped up beside Sarah and took her hand. "I have an announcement to make. I've asked Sarah to marry me. She has agreed, and she will be a part of our family as soon as we reach Dawson."

Hetty felt her eyes widen and before she could stop herself, she gasped. "What? Oh, that's—that's—"

"A surprise?" Sarah laughed. "But you saw the ring Donnie gave me, the one I had to give back." She looked at Uncle Donall, her eyes teasing him. "He's promised me another when we get to Dawson."

Papa, Mrs. V, and Alma crowded around the couple to congratulate them, but Hetty couldn't help worrying how they were all going to get to Dawson.

"How much money do you have, Sarah?" Hetty asked.

"Hetty! That's very impolite," Mrs. Vasquez scolded. She probably wanted to know, too, but she never would have asked.

Maybe Hetty had some spunk left over from confronting Uncle Donall. She'd blurted out the question before she thought about how it would sound. "I'm sorry," she apologized.

"That's okay, Hetty. It's no secret that I've never had to worry about money." Sarah unrolled one of the tulle roses on her hat to show them what was hidden inside—money, lots of money. If each rose held the same amount, there were thousands of dollars. Sarah *could* help them.

No one knew what to say. Hetty just stared at the fortune decorating Sarah's hat. Off and on, Hetty had wondered if Sarah Lancaster could be their thief. But now Hetty knew Sarah had no need to steal anything. She could buy the world.

"Please, please, let me help. I've come to love you all very much." Sarah held out money to Papa. "If you think you have to, you can pay me back when you find gold."

Papa looked at Mrs. Vasquez. She nodded. Papa didn't need her permission, but he had always been one to get everyone's opinion about things. It came from being a reporter, Hetty thought. Reporters always say, *And how do you feel about this?* Most people usually answer. Mrs. Vasquez was speechless, but Hetty could see that she looked happy.

Hetty felt totally relieved. They could go on.

As it turned out, when Sarah and Uncle Donall came back from hiring Indian packers to carry their supplies over the pass, they said none of the packers would climb that day. Sarah seemed impatient with the delay, but even so, she sparkled with happiness, looking lovely in her pretty blue corduroy suit.

"Why won't they climb?" Hetty asked. "It's a beautiful day."

"They say there's too much new snow. It's not safe," Uncle Donall explained. "Even the Mounties are telling people not to climb today."

"We ran into Colin Brandauer," Sarah said. "He said to tell you hello, Hetty." Sarah clapped her hands. "I know. If we can't climb over the pass, we can at least go sledding. We can climb the stairs a short way, then sled down. Want to go, Donnie?"

Uncle Donall shook his head no, laughing at Sarah's foolishness. "I think I can find better recreation."

"Can we go, Mrs. V? Climb a little way and slide down?" Hetty begged. "Sledding looks like such fun."

Many Klondikers were on the Golden Stairs despite the warnings of the Native packers and the Mounties. Alongside the stairs, people returning to camp for a second load were sliding down on whatever they could find—shovels, goldpans, or the seat of their pants.

"Please, Mama," Alma begged. "I've never been sledding."

Mrs. V gave in, and Hetty and Alma took off. By the time they had dug their goldpans out of the supplies,

Sarah had disappeared, so Hetty and Alma raced to the Golden Stairs to find her.

Even with the sun shining, the air was cold. Hetty felt like a roly-poly bear in two sweaters, long underwear, two pairs of pants, her coat, and gloves with mittens pulled over them. She had tied a muffler over her stocking hat to keep it on tight.

Climbing was easier with no load on her back—but not any faster, since there was a Klondiker directly in front of her and one right in back of Alma. Each was bent double carrying sixty or eighty pounds. Hetty and Alma stepped up slowly, moving with the crowd. The stairs were steep and slick. Hetty clutched the rope that someone had strung all the way to the top for a banister. One step, one step, one step. Fifteen hundred steps would take all day.

Someone slid past them, squealing. "Look, it's Sarah, acting like a little kid," Alma laughed. "How'd she get so far ahead of us?"

"I'm getting scared, Alma. This is far enough. Let's step out of line." The mountainside had gotten so steep that Hetty found she couldn't look up or down without feeling dizzy.

She and Alma stepped off the stairs and sank into the deep snow. Hetty finally looked around. People who slid by were going fast, really fast. Now Hetty completely lost her nerve. She waited and waited, clutching her goldpan, and Alma waited with her, both of them turning to icicles. Hetty wiggled and stomped. She knew that she had to slide or climb, one or the other.

Soon Sarah waved at them and walked back to where they stood. "Are you scared? It's great fun, girls. Just shut your eyes and go. I'm going to climb farther up for one more slide. Then let's go have hot chocolate."

Hetty and Alma watched Sarah until she was out of sight. "Okay, we have to slide," Hetty said. She took a deep breath. "Ready, Alma? Let's hold hands. One, two—"

Before Hetty could say "three" and sit on her goldpan, a huge booming sound filled the air, echoing like the biggest clap of thunder she'd ever heard.

"Avalanche!" someone yelled. "Run!"

People on the stairs jumped off and slid past them. Hetty had time to look up once more before she was knocked off her feet.

Tons of snow raced toward them!

CHAPTER 12
DIGGING OUT

Hetty clutched the sides of her goldpan and slid ahead of the avalanche. She ducked her head, expecting to be buried. When she finally came to a stop at the bottom of the Golden Stairs, a terrible silence surrounded her.

Alma broke the quiet. "Sarah!" she screamed. "Sarah was above us, Hetty. I don't see her anywhere."

"She was right in the path of the snowslide."

Suddenly everyone came alive. Climbers who had escaped the snowslide hurried back up the mountain to help those who were buried.

"Hetty!" Uncle Donall scrambled up behind them and grabbed her. "Was Sarah with you? Sledding? She was, wasn't she?" He scanned the mountainside, fear etched on his face.

"She was above us, Uncle Donall. She must have been buried in the slide."

Uncle Donall grabbed a tin plate from the debris around them. “Where? Where? Show me where to dig.”

“I—I don’t know.” Hetty floundered in the deep-packed snow. She grabbed her goldpan. “She could be anywhere. But higher, higher up than this.”

Hetty and Alma followed Uncle Donall, digging their toes into snow packed tight like cement.

“There, look!” Hetty pointed to a scrap of blue corduroy sticking out of the snow.

They dug frantically, tugging at Sarah’s blue corduroy skirt, her high boots. When they had her uncovered, Hetty was even more frightened. Sarah’s eyes were closed, her lashes frosted. Her face was a deathly white, almost blue. Hetty couldn’t tell if she was breathing.

“Take her back to camp. Get her warm, Uncle Donall,” Hetty said as Uncle Donall lifted Sarah. Hetty finished digging Sarah’s hat out of the snow and held it tight.

“Come on, Hetty.” Alma tugged on Hetty’s sleeve. “Let’s get out of here. The snow might come down again.”

They half slid, half ran to the campground.

“We need hot tea and blankets, Mrs. V. Hurry.” Hetty held the tent flap so that Uncle Donall could carry Sarah inside.

“You make some tea, Alma,” Mrs. V said as she and Papa hurried into the tent. She helped Uncle Donall take off Sarah’s snow-caked suit.

They piled blankets around Sarah and tucked them in

tight. Papa and Uncle Donall stood watching, looking helpless and frightened.

Finally Sarah's eyes flew open. "What—where?" One arm slid from under the blankets as she reached up. "My hat—where's my hat?"

Hetty almost laughed with relief that Sarah was all right, and that the first thing she had thought of was her banking hat. "I found it, Sarah. It's right here beside you."

"Oh, Hetty, thank you." Then Sarah's eyes softened as she looked at Uncle Donall. Mrs. V, Papa, and Hetty slipped from the tent and joined Alma at the fire.

"Look," Alma said, pointing toward Chilkoot Pass.

Hetty squinted and saw people being carried down the mountain.

Fifteen bodies came down the mountain that day. Soon the sound of sawing and hammering—the sound of men making coffins—echoed across the otherwise silent blue sky.

The next morning Eddie came by their tent. "There's going to be a big funeral at ten o'clock. A man came to get my pa to play his accordion. You going, Hetty? Alma?"

"No, they're not," Mrs. Vasquez said.

"Yes, Maria, I think the girls should go. We should

all go," Papa said. "The world is full of good and bad. We can't protect the girls from seeing both."

Hetty knew Papa was right. Still, it was a sad morning for people who two days ago had been laughing and planning a future filled with big dreams.

At the service, Colin stood with the McKinley family. Hetty was relieved to know that he was safe. The coffins were buried in deep snow, the ground too frozen for graves to be dug. "We'll bury them in the ground next summer," Colin told them. "There's a bottle in each coffin with the name of the deceased so family can find their loved ones and put up a marker later."

The Reverend Mortimer, who had spoken over Rosie Jacobson's grave, gave the service, but Hetty heard little of what he said.

She looked at her family, thankful that they were all still alive. Sarah looked pale, but she had insisted on coming to the service. Uncle Donall stood beside her, his arm around her, holding her close. Mrs. Vasquez hugged Alma tight. Hetty snuggled against Papa's shoulder, hoping for something good to happen soon to balance out this sad day.

The happy news surprised them all. At noon, Sarah made the announcement. "Donnie and I realize how close we came to being separated. How lucky we were. We aren't going to wait until we get to Dawson to get married. We're going to get married on top of Chilkoot Pass." She turned and smiled at Uncle Donall.

Hetty had never seen him look so happy, and with such a silly smile on his face. She stopped worrying that Sarah Lancaster was so rich and Uncle Donall so poor. This was turning into a true fairy tale.

A wedding! A wedding atop Chilkoot Pass!

Chapter 13
A Fairy-Tale Wedding

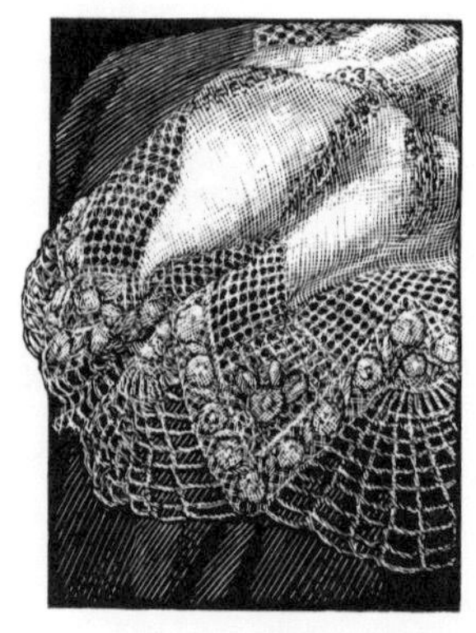

"Perhaps," Mrs. Vasquez said, "out of respect for those who died on the mountain, you two should wait to get married."

Sarah and Uncle Donall looked at each other, and Sarah nodded. "We'll talk to the Reverend Mortimer," Sarah said. "Get his opinion."

"I have to climb fifteen hundred stairs and still be able to stand up with Donall. In a few days, I'll be stronger," Papa added.

"A bride needs time to get ready for her wedding. And I'll admit to feeling a little shaky myself," Sarah told Uncle Donall.

By the next morning, Sarah and Uncle Donall had finished their plans. "The Reverend Mortimer said he would marry us day after tomorrow at the summit of the mountain," Sarah told them at breakfast. "He said if we waited two or three days, he thought people would understand, and that a wedding might help lift people's spirits. I'm so glad he's not old-fashioned, wanting us to wait for months. I have my heart set on a wedding on Chilkoot Pass."

Hetty had never been around anyone who was getting married. Inside their tent, now forbidden territory to the men, she and Alma watched Sarah and Mrs. V make wedding preparations and helped when they could.

"This is nearly white." Sarah held up a dress that she had dug out of her trunk. "Do you think it will be all right for a wedding dress?"

Mrs. Vasquez, Hetty, and Alma carefully ran their hands over the soft cotton and lace. They watched as Sarah slipped it over her head. She had on all her petticoats, and the skirt flared out as she twirled.

"You're going to freeze," Hetty said.

"I'll wear my coat until the very last minute." Sarah laughed. For most of the trip, Sarah Lancaster had been laughing, and now her face glowed with excitement and happiness. Sarah really did love Uncle Donall, Hetty realized. Hetty felt happy for them both.

"I've just remembered." Mrs. Vasquez ran to dig into her own trunk. "I have some lace curtains I brought for my house in Dawson. It will probably be a one-room shack, but lace curtains will make it feel like home. You can wear one, Sarah, for a veil. You can't be a bride without a veil."

Sarah clapped her hands. Mrs. Vasquez dumped everything out of her trunk to find the curtains on the very bottom. She pulled one out, carefully unfolded it, smoothed out the wrinkles, and draped it over Sarah's head.

Hetty laughed. "What a miracle that you didn't lose your hat in the avalanche. Are you going to wear it for the wedding?" She knew what Sarah's answer would be. Hetty smiled every time she thought about Sarah's hat. Her banking hat, her treasure hat. Who would have ever guessed?

"Of course. We'll drape the veil over the hat."

"You have to have something old," Hetty said, remembering the traditional rhyme for brides.

"My dress—my dress is old." Sarah twirled around again.

"And something new," Alma added.

"Oh, dear, where can I get something new?"

"Something borrowed," Alma continued. "Well, you're only borrowing Mama's curtain. She'll want it back."

"And something blue." Hetty dug in her pack. "I have a blue handkerchief here someplace. I sewed the lace on it myself—not too well, I'm afraid. I'm terrible with sewing." She found the handkerchief and pressed it into Sarah's hand.

"Hetty, Alma, can I come in?" Eddie called from outside the tent.

"No! Don't you dare, Eddie Jacobson." Hetty giggled.

"But, Eddie," Sarah called, "will you ask your father if he'll play his accordion for my wedding?"

"Girls, bah!" Eddie said.

Hetty stuck her head out of the tent. "Please, Eddie, go ask him."

Sarah's happy mood was catching. Mrs. Vasquez and Andy Nickerson made plans for Uncle Donall and Sarah's wedding feast at the top of the pass. Mrs. V said they would set up the second tent for the wedding couple to start their honeymoon.

"You and Alma will wear your best dresses, of course," Sarah said to Hetty the next morning. "You and Alma are my bridesmaids. I won't have it any other way. At home, I would have had half a dozen bridesmaids, but you two are so special, you'll make up for that. And Mrs. V, you are the matron of honor." Sarah leaned close to Mrs. Vasquez and whispered, "Unless you want to have a double wedding." She winked at Hetty and Alma.

"Oh, my goodness, of course not." Mrs. Vasquez ducked her head and headed for her stove to flip over some sourdough pancakes.

"Do you think Mama will marry Mr. Nickerson someday?" Alma whispered.

"I don't know. I think she likes him, and he certainly likes her, but get married? I don't know."

The morning of the wedding was cold but clear—not even a hint of a cloud. Everyone was too excited to eat much breakfast. Mrs. V, Hetty, and Alma packed up the kitchen supplies and all but the few personal items they were going to carry themselves. Uncle Donall and Papa finished organizing the rest of their provisions for the Native packers, who had arrived at the McKinley camp. The tent was still standing, because Sarah was getting dressed.

Mrs. V had suggested that Sarah put on her wedding dress after she climbed the stairs, but Sarah said that wouldn't be any fun. Instead of strolling down a church aisle, she was marching up golden stairs. She had agreed, however, to putting her dress shoes—high-button high heels of white kid leather—in her pack to change into at the top. Uncle Donall would have to see his bride in her wedding clothes before the ceremony, of course—even if it was supposed to be bad luck. Hetty hoped that they'd already had all the bad luck they would ever have.

The Jacobsons came over right after breakfast to lend a hand with the preparations and accompany the wedding party up the Golden Stairs. Hetty's heart went out to Mrs. Jacobson, who helped where she could. She looked so sad, even though she was trying to smile past the tears in her eyes. She was surely thinking about baby Rosie, who would never grow up and get married. Hetty tried not to dwell on the past. They had to go forward.

Mr. Jacobson played hymns and old melodies while everyone stood around the dying embers of the morning's campfire, waiting for Sarah and Mrs. V to finish getting ready. Eddie was unusually quiet, probably not knowing what to say or do, since weddings were "girl stuff," and Carl stood staring at the Golden Stairs. Hetty knew they were still sad about losing their baby sister, too.

Hetty and Alma, with nothing to do, bounced and whispered, wishing they could get started.

Suddenly Moosejaw rounded the tent, a big grin on his face. "Where's the blushing bride?" In his arms he carried what looked like a huge white rabbit. "When I heard about the wedding, I found a Native woman who was selling these Arctic hare fur coats. Here's my gift for Sarah, Hetty. Is she in the tent? Will you and Alma take it to her?"

Hetty and Alma took the soft fur coat from him. It was so long, they had to carry it together as they stepped into the tent.

"Here, Sarah," Hetty said. "Something new! Moosejaw brought it. You can wear this over your wedding dress. You'll be wonderfully warm. The coat will come to your boots."

Sarah squealed and reached for the coat. They handed it to her and Mrs. Vasquez. Sarah reached out of the tent and grabbed Moosejaw's hand, then pulled him all the way into the tent and hugged him. "Oh, Moosejaw, this must have cost you an entire bag of gold dust."

Moosejaw's face turned bright red. "The truth is, I

knew the woman, and she didn't charge me *cheechako* prices. Please, I want you to have it."

Hetty and Alma followed Moosejaw back outside. Then Mrs. Vasquez stuck her head out of the tent. "Sarah is almost ready. She says you men should go on to the bottom of the stairs and wait for her. She needs a moment to catch her breath."

As they left, all the men were laughing and teasing Uncle Donall, who hadn't said a word that Hetty had heard this morning. She smiled to think that he might be scared.

When the men had left, Sarah stepped out of the tent and took a huge breath, almost a sigh. "Oh, my goodness, I'm so nervous."

"You look so pretty!" Hetty clapped her hands.

Sarah's white fur coat hung open slightly to reveal the lacy white dress. The picture hat was in place, draped with Mrs. V's lace curtain. Sarah wore her hair down, and it fell almost to her waist. A few curly tendrils framed her beaming face. She kept pushing them out of the way with her white kid gloves.

"Isn't your face supposed to be covered with the veil?" Hetty asked.

"That's the tradition, but I don't want to fall off the stairs and slide all the way to the bottom."

Sophie Jacobson stepped up to Sarah. "I'd be honored if you'd carry my white Bible, Sarah." Sophie placed the book in Sarah's hands. "Since you have no bridal bouquet, unless you take those flowers off your hat."

Sarah smiled at Hetty. "I don't think I'll do that." She took Sophie's hand. "Thank you, Sophie, it's an honor to carry your Bible. It looks old."

"I've had it since I was a little girl. I meant to give it to Rosie someday for her wedding."

Sarah leaned over and kissed Mrs. Jacobson on the cheek. "Now, stop fussing over me. Let me look at my bridesmaids."

Sarah stood Hetty and Alma in front of her and looked them over. Hetty rubbed her locket and hoped she looked good enough for a wedding.

"Perfect. I'm so glad you found your locket, Hetty," Sarah said. "You *both* look perfect—except for one thing. This is a special occasion, and I must admit we probably don't any of us smell our best." She giggled, reminding them of the sponge baths they were taking now that hot water was scarce. "Hetty, I have a small bottle of French perfume tucked away. Not for a wedding—not for *my* wedding, goodness knows. When I planned this trip, I never imagined this. I just thought about parties. Will you go get it while I make sure I'm ready?"

French perfume! Hetty laughed as she ducked back into the tent. All of Sarah's things were gone except for Sarah's small pack and a white drawstring purse that Sarah usually carried at her waist. The perfume had to be in one of them.

Hetty selected the pack. Inside were more drawstring bags. Eenie, meeny, miney—

Hetty lifted out a large plaid bag. She pulled at the strings of the pouch. Then she felt her heart sink in her chest. All her breath flew out in a *whoosh.*

Here was Mr. Nickerson's skinning knife in its leather sheath. She recognized an initial, a curly *M* embroidered in satin on a white napkin. Belinda Mulrooney's linen napkin, and—and—

Papa's watch. Mrs. Vasquez's brooch. Miss Pittypat. The two photographs from Dyea Beach. And Hetty was sure that, until recently, her locket had been here, too.

Sarah Lancaster—Sarah, the laughing bride, Hetty's new aunt-to-be—was their thief!

CHAPTER 14
CONFRONTING THE THIEF

Hetty's heart pounded in her ears. She bent over and took a deep breath. What should she do? Uncle Donall was happier than Hetty had ever seen him. Everyone they knew, and many people they didn't know, were excited and waiting to celebrate with Uncle Donall and Sarah. Could Hetty let Uncle Donall marry a thief? But—Uncle Donall was also a thief. Even though he had returned the money and apologized to Mrs. Vasquez, he had still stolen from her. Hetty felt terribly confused.

A picture flashed through her mind of the awful flogging she had seen in Sheep Camp. Would someone take a whip to Sarah Lancaster if Hetty told she was a thief?

"Hetty? Did you find it? Come on. I'm ready to leave," Sarah called to Hetty from outside the tent. Hetty had to do something. Or nothing.

Quickly she placed everything back in the pouch and

pulled the drawstring closed. She stuffed the pouch back into Sarah's pack. Then she grabbed the smaller bag that Sarah carried for a purse. Sure enough, there was a tiny bottle of perfume at the bottom of the bag.

Running out of the tent, she handed the purse and the bottle to Sarah without looking at her. She knew that Sarah would see in her eyes that something was wrong. She closed her eyes as Sarah leaned toward her and dabbed the sweet-smelling liquid behind each ear. The perfume was cloying, making her not want to take a deep breath.

"What's wrong, Hetty?" Alma whispered, taking hold of Hetty's arm. "Are you faint? The perfume is really strong, isn't it? I'm about to sneeze. Is it something else?" Alma rattled on, excited.

"I—I'll tell you later."

A Native woman arrived to pack up the tent. Quickly, Mrs. Vasquez gave her some last-minute instructions.

Mrs. V, Sophie Jacobson, Hetty, and Alma walked with Sarah until she met Uncle Donall and Papa at the bottom of the Golden Stairs. It could—it *should*—have been a fairy-tale wedding party. Hetty wanted to collapse in the snow and cry.

Instead, she stepped into line on the Golden Stairs. The minister, Uncle Donall, and Sarah went first, followed by Papa and Mr. Jacobson, then Mrs. Vasquez, Hetty and Alma, and the rest of the Jacobson family. Ahead of the wedding party, on and on up the towering mountain, a stream of people walked, getting smaller and smaller in the distance like a trail of ants. Up, up, up everyone climbed, one step at a time, hardly looking around at the beauty of the mountain. Hetty set her feet firmly on the icy steps, seeing only the boots ahead of her.

In Hetty's mind, a memory of the roar of the avalanche played over and over in the bright, crisp mountain air. *No, not again,* Hetty told herself. *Not today*. She forced herself to breathe slowly and deeply. She had to keep up, she had to keep going. She dared not count, nor think about fifteen hundred steps. She clutched the rope banister to keep from stumbling when her legs ached and felt rubbery.

Finally, late in the afternoon, they reached the top. All of them stepped away from the staircase and fell silent, looking with wonder and awe at the snow-covered mountain ranges beyond the pass, silhouetted against the blue, blue sky. Down the trail, far in the distance, lay Lake Lindeman, where they would camp for the winter and build a boat. Hetty counted seven glaciers, the sun glancing off the ice, creating rainbows that seemed to dance across the snow.

"My God, how beautiful you have made the world," Mrs. Vasquez whispered.

Mr. Jacobson started playing the wedding march from *Lohengrin.* Sarah, now wearing her pretty shoes, hooked her arm into Uncle Donall's and the couple walked to stand before the Reverend Christopher Mortimer. Hetty,

Alma, and Mrs. Vasquez stood on one side of Sarah. Papa stood beside Uncle Donall.

Hetty hardly heard the vows. Her thoughts overwhelmed her.

"The ring?" asked the Reverend Mortimer, looking at Papa.

Papa reached into his pocket and handed a gold ring to Uncle Donall. After Uncle Donall slid it on her finger, Sarah held her hand out in front of her. The ring gleamed in the fading light. Hetty could see that it was made from tiny gold nuggets melted together into a single band. Where had Uncle Donall gotten another ring?

Hetty was numb for the next hour. She helped with the party. She listened to the buzz of conversation around her, the laughter, the happy music Mr. Jacobson played. She watched people, total strangers, congratulating Sarah and Uncle Donall.

"Hetty?" Alma put her hand on Hetty's arm.

"Don't." Hetty pushed Alma's hand away. "Never mind."

"Something's wrong, Hetty. I know it is."

"I can't tell you now. Come on, your mother needs us."

Just then, Sarah came to Hetty and took her hand. "Hetty, will you help me? If I don't get this corset off, I'm going to faint. I need your help."

"Mrs. Vasquez can unlace it."

"I want you to help me, Hetty. Come on." Sarah tugged Hetty into the tent set away from the trail, the tent where Uncle Donall and Sarah Lancaster—now Sarah McKinley—would spend their wedding night.

"I lied. I haven't worn a corset for a single day of this whole trip." Sarah put her arm around Hetty. "Now, what's the matter? Didn't you want your Uncle Donall to get married? Are you jealous? You can't be jealous, Hetty," Sarah teased her.

Hetty burst into tears. But that didn't keep her from reaching for Sarah's pack, propped against the tent pole. Hetty reached in, pulled out the plaid pouch, and began to untie the string.

"Oh, don't, Hetty." Sarah tried to stop her. "That's—"

"All the things you've stolen?" Hetty found her voice. "How could you? Oh, Sarah, how could you steal from all of us? You said we were your family. You said you loved us."

Hetty rubbed her locket and kept her fingers around it. *Help me, Mama. Help me know what to do.*

"I'm—I'm so sorry you found those things, Hetty."

"I'm sure you are."

"You don't understand. I was going to return every item. I took them—well, I took all of them before I knew you, before I called you family. Before I understood what these things meant to you. But now I do. I was going to slip them back into your packs, just like I slipped them out. I started by returning your locket." Sarah leaned on a stack of flour and sugar bags and stared at her hands, her new ring.

"But why? Why did you take them, Sarah? None of them are worth much, if anything, except to the people they belonged to."

Hetty let the silence grow. She could feel how uncomfortable Sarah was, maybe even how sorry she was. But that didn't make what she had done right.

"It—it was just a game," Sarah said finally. Her voice was almost a whisper.

"A *game*?"

"I don't know how to make you understand. I had a silly group of friends in San Francisco who dared me to come to the Yukon. Then they gave me a game to play—a scavenger hunt."

"A scavenger hunt?" Hetty struggled to understand.

"Yes." Sarah couldn't meet Hetty's eyes. "The game was the latest rage. We made up lists of things and dropped the lists in a hat. Teams, or sometimes individuals, would draw out a list. Then they'd have to go all over the city to find the ridiculous and impossible items. Afterward, we'd have a party and give prizes to the people who found the most items on their list. A party was planned for me in San Francisco when I returned from the Yukon. I'd have to show that I came back with everything on my list to win my prize."

"You were going to get a prize for *stealing*?" Hetty tried to imagine this game that the rich young people on Nob Hill had enjoyed playing with their friends.

"It's *not* stealing, Hetty. It's borrowing. Or sometimes begging something from someone. One of the things on my list was a famous person's autograph. I got Jack London to sign my book, hoping he'd be a famous writer someday."

"What else was on your list?" Hetty still didn't understand, or forgive Sarah, but curiosity got the best of her.

"A necklace. A photograph. A lady's pin. A man's watch. A knife. Something from a hotel where I stayed. I took a napkin from Belinda Mulrooney. She had so many. And I haven't stayed in her hotel yet, but I'm sure I will when we get to Dawson. They were mostly all little things, things that weren't worth much, that were fun, but didn't matter—"

"These things mattered to us. Mrs. V's husband gave her this brooch. Alma's father gave her Miss Pittypat. He brought it back from China."

Sarah took a deep breath. "I—I realize all that now, Hetty. You're helping me see that some things represent people and memories, wonderful memories." Sarah took both Hetty's hands. "I'm not that same silly girl who left San Francisco such a short time ago. The one who did nothing but go to parties and play games. Who could never pass up a bet. Can you believe that, Hetty? You have to believe it. You have to forgive me."

Sarah put her hand under Hetty's chin and made Hetty look at her. There were tears in Sarah's green eyes. And she looked sincere. But—

"I never had anything like your locket, Hetty. Nothing

from my parents, who died when I was a baby. Nothing that mattered to me. Oh, I had things, all the things I wanted. I was rich, spoiled—very spoiled, I realize now. I love my grandparents, but Hetty, I've not ever had any friends, any good friends that mattered to me. You matter to me now. You and Mrs. Vasquez, your papa, and Donnie. I love your Uncle Donall, Hetty. You have to believe me. You have to give me a second chance."

Hetty shut her eyes and took several deep breaths. She wanted to forgive Sarah. She wanted this to be over, to put all this behind her.

She made her voice very tough, very hard. "I will forgive you, Sarah. I can forgive you on one condition."

"What? Just tell me, Hetty. Tell me."

"You return everything you took." Hetty held Sarah's eyes.

"Oh, yes, of course."

"And you apologize to the owner."

Sarah hesitated. "Now? Right now?"

"Now," Hetty demanded. "Right now. This is your chance to start over with your new family."

Now Sarah cried. Maybe some of the emotion came from getting married, from the excitement of the day, from all that had happened the last few days. After all, Sarah had nearly died in the avalanche.

Hetty put her arms around Sarah and held her close. When she finally stopped sobbing, Sarah hugged back.

Uncle Donall stuck his head in the tent. His blue eyes sparkled. "Where's the happy bride? Why are you crying, Sarah? Have you changed your mind? Too late." Uncle Donall stepped into the tent and took Sarah away from Hetty.

She kept sniffing for a minute, using Hetty's blue handkerchief to wipe her face. "Will you ask all the family to gather together for a few minutes, Donall? Before we finish the party? To have a toast. Just family, including the Vasquezes, of course, and Mr. Nickerson. Who might be family soon, too."

Sarah had recovered enough to make a joke. She smiled sadly at Hetty. "Wouldn't that be funny? But Mrs. V missed her chance for a wedding on Chilkoot Pass."

Soon Uncle Donall had gathered the family together. In their small circle, away from the crowd, Sarah Lancaster McKinley took time from her wedding celebration to set some things in order. Hetty held the pouch of stolen items while Sarah returned them and apologized to each owner.

Papa's mouth fell open as he took his watch and stared at it. Mr. Nickerson smiled his crooked smile, took his wicked-looking skinning knife from its sheath, and tested the edge to see if it was still sharp.

Probably, like Hetty, no one knew what to say or even what to think of Sarah's having taken all their things. Maybe they'd talk it over later, but now they received each missing item and nodded at Sarah as she said she was sorry, so sorry for taking it.

"I can forgive her, Hetty," Alma said in a quiet voice as she ran her finger over her doll's painted china hair. "She took good care of Miss Pittypat. But can you believe she took these things? Can you forgive her?"

"In time, Alma. I think I can in time." Hetty fingered the cold surface of her locket. She tucked it inside her blouse beneath all the sweaters she'd pulled on as the day darkened and stars popped out.

Hetty heard Mr. Jacobson begin the first notes of a waltz. Uncle Donall took Sarah's arm and led her back to the party. Mrs. Vasquez, standing beside Hetty and Alma, watched the wedding couple go. She shook her head and smiled. "Birds of a feather," she whispered.

Somehow that old saying struck Hetty as terribly funny. Her playful, irresponsible Uncle Donall and the playful, rich society girl from Nob Hill made a matched pair. But Hetty believed in her heart that they really were changing. Sarah wasn't the spoiled girl they had met at Dyea. Loving someone always changes a person. This trip was changing all their lives, Hetty realized, but maybe it had changed Sarah's life most of all.

Hetty took a deep breath and looked up. "Mrs V, what's that?" She pointed to the northern sky.

In the distance, yellow, pink, blue, and green lights danced from behind the mountains as if celebrating the wedding with them.

"Northern lights," Andy Nickerson said, stepping up

behind them to ask Mrs. V if she would dance with him. "Dancing spirits. A good sign."

Hetty could scarcely believe the light show in the sky. She imagined how she would describe the colors in her journal. She thought about how she would describe this day—a day that had brought a new member into their family.

They had reached the mountain pass, an almost impossible trip, Hetty realized as she looked back on the journey so far. She knew they'd make it to Dawson to look for gold.

But Hetty found that she didn't care about gold. In a way, she thought, she and Sarah Lancaster had learned the same thing on this trip. Hetty wondered if she could even explain it in words. Back in San Francisco, her greatest wish had been for a house. Now she knew that anyplace could hold a family, even a tent on the side of a mountain. Family and friends were what was true gold.

Hetty had been sure she needed a desk to write good stories. She knew now that she could write sitting on a log, on a rock, inside a tent in a snowstorm.

And now she had something to write about. My, did she have stories to tell—stories about how she had walked, climbed, scrambled to the top of the world, her family and friends by her side. And even the sky lit up with their celebration.

1897

A Peek into the Past

Looking Back: 1897

Klondikers arriving in Dyea, Alaska, at the height of the gold rush

In 1897, when Hetty's story takes place, the United States was in a severe depression. Many people were out of work. So when, on July 14, miners arrived in San Francisco Bay on the ship *Excelsior,* announcing gold nuggets in the Yukon the size of potatoes, excitement spread like a summer grass fire.

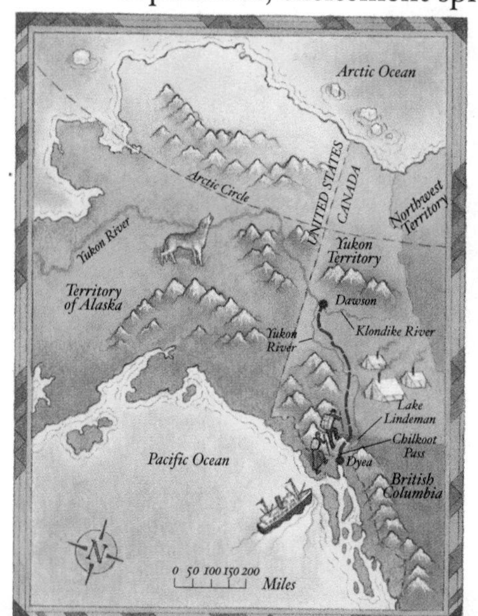

The red line shows the 500-mile route from Dyea, Alaska, to the goldfields in Canada's Yukon Territory.

Some Americans had heard of Alaska, land the United States had purchased from Russia 30 years before. But until that July day, almost no one had heard of the remote Canadian territory called the Yukon.

Yet, just like Hetty's papa, people all across America quit their jobs, sold their homes, and rushed north to make their fortunes. They became known as "Klondikers," after the river where gold was first discovered. During the winter of 1897-98, more than 30,000 gold seekers stampeded to the Yukon.

Most Klondikers traveled by steamship to Alaska, landing at frontier outposts like Dyea. Then the real adventure began, as they faced the challenge of making their way 500 miles north to the goldfields. The first 17 miles—from the Alaskan coast up rugged mountains to the Canadian border—was the hardest stretch of the entire trip. Most Klondikers followed the trail that Hetty's family takes, crossing into Canada at Chilkoot Pass.

Goods were so scarce in the Yukon that Klondikers had to haul in enough supplies to last a year—nearly a ton per person, including everything from flour, sugar, beans, and bacon to tents, frying pans, shovels, and axes. By the spring of 1898, Northwest Mounted Police were stationed at Chilkoot Pass to collect taxes on the goods Klondikers brought in. They turned away anyone who hadn't brought enough supplies—or enough money to pay taxes.

The final ascent to Chilkoot Pass was called the Golden Stairs, because the trail consisted of 1,500 steps carved out of the ice and snow. It was extremely steep and treacherous—

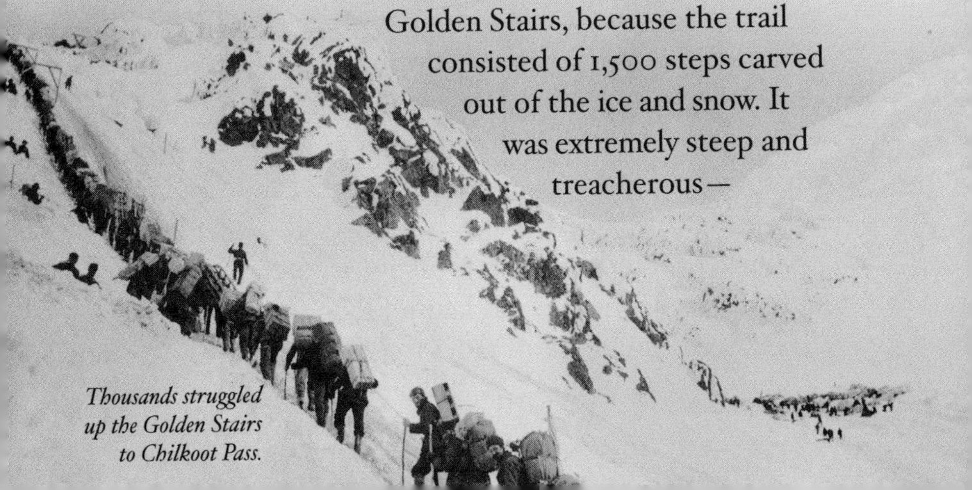

Thousands struggled up the Golden Stairs to Chilkoot Pass.

A family heading out from Dyea with one of their many loads of supplies

and people had to make as many as 30 trips up the stairs to haul all their supplies to the pass.

People carried strange items on the trail: musical instruments, turkeys, grinding stones, bolts of cloth, sewing machines, even a 125-pound plow. Some realized the items they carried were foolish and left them when the trail got steeper.

Only a few children made the trip, but many women went. Most were wives or sweethearts, but single women like Sarah Lancaster also sought fortune or adventure in the Yukon. Since it wasn't considered proper for women to wear trousers, they made the trek in skirts or dresses. One woman, like Sarah, wore a rose-covered picture hat the entire way.

Reaching Chilkoot Pass, as Hetty's party did, was a tremendous accomplishment. Many Klondikers, exhausted and discouraged, gave up and headed home long before they reached the pass. Many others died along the trail of accidents, pneumonia, diphtheria, spinal meningitis, and food poisoning.

Once Klondikers got to Chilkoot Pass, the hardest part of the trip was behind them—but they still had hundreds of miles to go! From the

Two women Klondikers, dressed for the trail in heavy coats and boots

pass, Klondikers hiked down the mountain to Lake Lindeman, where they camped through the winter. While they waited for the ice on the rivers to break up, they cut timber and built boats to take them farther north.

When the ice broke on May 29, 1898, thousands continued their trip by river to Dawson, the main town in the Yukon. Some boats, poorly built, broke up in the river rapids, and people drowned.

Those who made it to Dawson discovered that finding gold was incredibly hard work. All the nuggets lying on top of the ground had already been picked up, so the Klondikers had to dig for gold. In winter, when temperatures reached -50 to -70 degrees and the ground was frozen solid, miners set fires to thaw the top layer of earth, scraped it off, then repeated the process. In summer, they *panned* the piled-up dirt for gold. They put the dirt, bit by bit, in pans or wooden bins, then ran creek water through. The soil washed away, but any flakes of gold settled to the bottom of the pan. This was a slow and tedious way to make a few dollars.

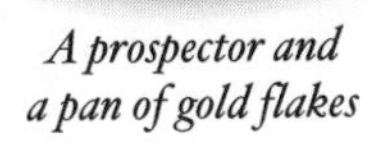

A prospector and a pan of gold flakes

A "four-dollar pan" was considered excellent. In 1897, a restaurant meal in the States cost 25¢. A four-room apartment rented for $1.25 a week.

Prices were much higher in the Yukon, however. Supplies grew scarce as miners flooded into Dawson with gold, but little else. Apples cost $1 apiece. Eggs, not all fresh, went for $18 a dozen. Milk was $30 a gallon, and brooms were $17 apiece. A kitten, to keep a lonely miner company, cost an ounce of gold, $17. A man carried a Seattle newspaper to Dawson and sold it to a miner for $50.

Some Klondikers made their fortunes in other ways than digging for gold. Belinda Mulrooney was a real woman who made her fortune running a hotel in Dawson. Other women got rich operating restaurants or by sewing or washing for miners. Laundry women could find as much as $20 in gold dust in their washtubs at the end of a day! Some single women became dance-hall girls. Men paid $1 to dance with them for 15 minutes.

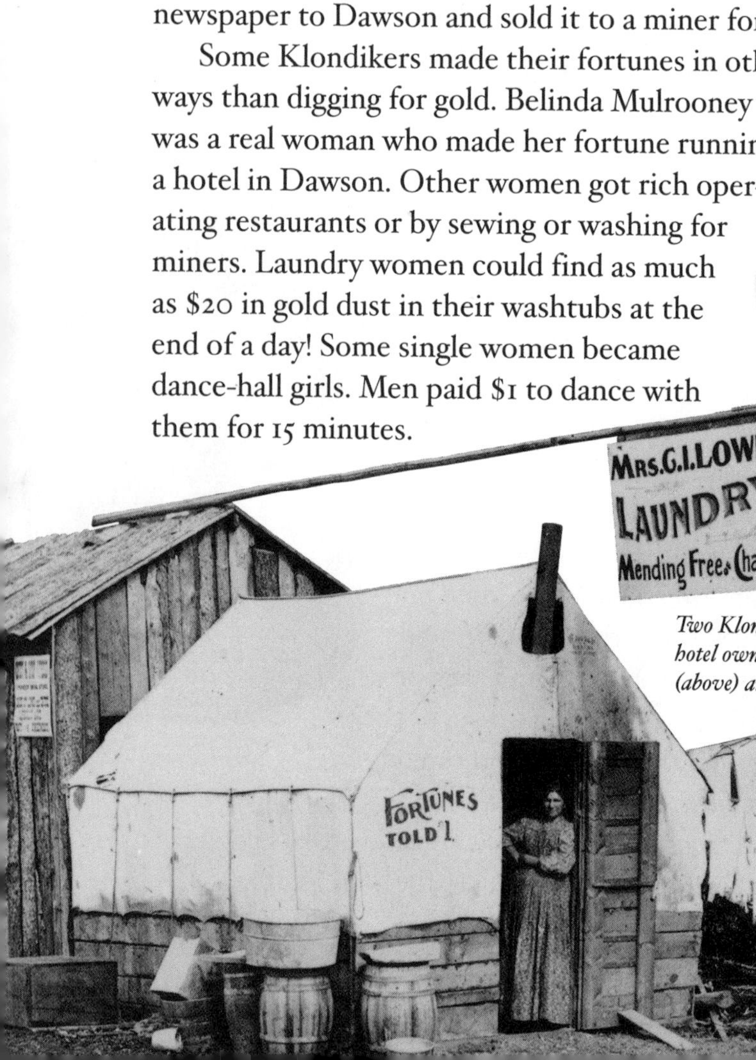

Two Klondike businesswomen: hotel owner Belinda Mulrooney (above) and a laundress

Jack London became famous for his novels and stories set in the Yukon wilderness.

Still other Yukoners found their fortune not in dollars but in the adventures and stories they collected on their journey. That was surely true of the writer Jack London, who went to the Yukon in 1897 as a young man of 21. Though he spent less than a year there, London wrote, "It was in the Klondike I found myself." His best-known novels, *The Call of the Wild* and *White Fang,* and many of his short stories tell of the hardships, loneliness, and grandeur of the far north.

The gold rush lasted for only a couple of years. Few Klondikers found enough gold to get rich. Some who loved the rugged north settled in Canada or Alaska. But most, like Jack London, eventually returned home. Yet nearly all—like Hetty and her companions—found that their lives were forever changed by their journey to the Yukon.

AUTHOR'S NOTE

For Hetty's story, I have taken some liberties with historical events. Snow avalanches, like the one Hetty experiences, rarely occur along the Chilkoot Trail in autumn. However, on September 18, 1897, a flood and mud slide started at Stone House and continued to Sheep Camp, wiping out people's camps and provisions.

Snow avalanches are a danger on the Chilkoot Trail, though, especially in spring—as some unlucky Klondikers discovered. On April 2, 1898, five feet of heavy, wet snow fell in a few hours. Fierce winds piled up 70-foot drifts. On April 3, Palm Sunday, despite warnings from Native people that the snow was unstable, Klondikers started up the Golden Stairs. The snow avalanched, killing 60 men and women.

The colorful people whom Hetty meets on the trail are all taken from historical records, though probably no single traveler would have met them all. Jack London climbed the Chilkoot Pass in the fall of 1897 and reached Dawson before the lakes and rivers froze up. The Klondike's colorful people fill his stories.

I have given Andy Nickerson (Moosejaw) a larger part in Hetty's story than he had in the anecdote I read about him.

A group of Scottish men climbed Chilkoot Trail with bagpipes, and a young couple really did marry on Chilkoot Pass.

About the Author

Barbara Steiner started writing stories and poetry when she was eight years old. Her favorite books were mysteries, and sometimes, all alone in a big house, she'd scare herself reading.

She was attracted to the Klondike story not by the gold rush but by the challenge of climbing Chilkoot Pass. She has hiked and backpacked all over the world, including New Zealand, Australia, Kenya, and Hawaii. She has ridden elephants in India and climbed into tombs in Egypt. She has claustrophobia but loves to explore caves. Her motto is, "Do something once a year that scares you."

She has published many books for children and young adults. Her book *Ghost Cave,* set in her home state of Arkansas, was nominated for the 1990 Edgar Allan Poe Award for Best Children's Mystery. She now lives in Boulder, Colorado, with her husband and three cats.